Promises

A Novel
By Casey Curry

Dedication

This book is dedicated to my husband Bruce, who always sees the potential and promise in the storms, and to all of "Mufaro's Beautiful Daughters."

"A promise is a cloud. Fulfillment is rain."

~ Arabian Proverb

Part I

SPRING

The Promise of Pleasure

Chapter 1

....

Everyone in sight was in motion. The expansive lawn echoed spring and a huge white tent stood stoically in the center of it as two small women quickly moved a ladder along the inside ceiling, hanging huge dangling crystals. They clanked and rattled as if sounding a soft alarm. Several men placed large parquet squares together to create a dance floor. The air was warm and a slight breeze blew over the Severn River as the six middle- aged men in matching green pants and perspiration -stained shirts placed gold chivari chairs around metal-legged round tables with worn wooden tops.

Fifty-five–year -old Pam Sloane Hamilton watched for a moment. She stood out from the blur of motion for two reasons. The first was that she was the only person on the lawn not moving. The second was the way she was dressed. In a sea of uniforms, Pam stood 5'10" in a sage green sleeveless linen dress, her waist cinched with an oversized chocolate leather belt. Her silver David Yurman bracelets and matching earrings made her honey skin look even softer than it was. Her neat chin-length sepia bob didn't move. Pamela Hamilton had a presence that she was acutely aware of. She was meticulously groomed and always turned heads. The curves were all in the right places, and approaching sixty in five years didn't matter. Her look, simply stated, said "I don't need you."

The hand that held the fragile champagne flute filled with her lifesaving morning mimosa was the only thing moving on her body. Staring at the workers, she was reminded of her father and the way he worked so many decent backbreaking jobs to get her and her older sister, Ella Jean to college. She thought Daddy Sloane would be very proud of her today.

Pam's bright red full lips formed a faint smile as she wondered what he would think of the extravagance of his granddaughter's wedding. He died following a stroke six months after she married her husband, Randolph, so he never laid eyes on any of their four daughters. Pure sweetness danced over her soft amber face as she thought of her father. He loved her and believed in her and saved her from her mother's insanity. She quickly pushed all thoughts of her father out of her mind as they invariably led to thoughts of her mother and that led to anger and tears. Today was René's wedding and she didn't have time for rehashing her traumatic childhood. The girls would be up and stirring soon and the cake still hadn't arrived.

"What's the last word on the bakery situation?" Pam asked the tall lanky young woman wearing a madras plaid straight skirt with a peach twin sweater set. Completing the uniform was a simple strand of pearls and soft leather ballet flats. It was what she had worn each time she and Pam met to work on the details of the wedding this past year. It was always the same conservative outfit in a variety of understated hues. She squirmed nervously and did not make eye contact with Pam; instead she stared off to the left of her head. Shayla moved strands of her thick red hair from her face and winced. "I'm not sure, Mrs. Hamilton; I just called and got no answer."

"I need to know where they are and their estimated time of arrival, so get on it." Pam turned on her chocolate Jimmy Choo low-heeled pumps and walked towards the Officers' Club beyond the tent. An inconsiderate pain began in her temples as she thought about the thousands of dollars they were paying Annapolis' premier wedding planner, Miss Shayla McNair. Pam mumbled softly, "No answer my butt, find the darn cake."

The door of the O' Club opened revealing yards and yards of cream chiffon draping the walls, wainscoting and high ceilings. A round man approached her smelling of sweet cigars. His red skin wrinkled from a life lived outdoors. Phillip was the manager of the club and knew everything and everybody.

"Good morning, Mrs. Hamilton. We are ready to go and I see Rick has already gotten you a drink. Let me take the liberty of freshening it up for you." Pam acknowledged his greeting with a weary smile, extended the glass weakly and watched Phillip fill the half empty flute with bubbling champagne. He wasn't the bartender, he was the club manager. He rarely poured drinks and she knew the refill was as much for him as it was for her. A relaxed and happy Mrs. Hamilton would be less of a pain in his ass but a drunken Mrs. Hamilton would be even worse. Phillip knew all too how stressful a wedding could be for the mother-of-the bride. He admired and liked her, so he watched both Pam and her glass.

Pam reached in her pocket for her phone and punched in the number with quick deliberate finger jabs. Randolph picked up on the first ring.

"Good morning, honey, how are things going over there? Is the $10,000 red head whipping the perfect wedding together?" Randolph was playful in tone but dead serious in meaning. "Hardly," Pam rested the generic champagne flute on the counter and pressed three fingers firmly against her temple. Her head was now pounding. "Baby, it's a hot mess over here, but she still has five hours before the ceremony so I'm going to walk back home and give her space to do what we hired her to do. Is anybody up and stirring yet?"

Randolph chuckled. "Stop worrying, Pam, its 8 o'clock in the morning. I don't think anyone is up. I had a banana and read the paper. Things are pretty quiet. Take off your cape and tights and that big old "S" off your chest and come home, hon. My suggestion is that you enjoy the calm before the storm."

"Okay, I'm on my way." Pam placed the phone back in her pocket and pushed the champagne flute to the center of the counter. She looked around for Phillip to say goodbye. No sign of him. Walking out the door, she blocked the sun from her eyes with the curve of a hand over her brow while searching the sea of workers for Shayla. She was on the phone looking stressed and intense. Pam hoped she was talking to the baker but decided not to inquire any further. She waved to Shayla and walked briskly across the lawn to their quarters on Porter.

Six gray houses stood in a neat row wearing navy blue and white striped awnings as if they were hats. Captain's Row was where the senior officers lived during their two to three year tours at the Naval Academy. They wore the rank of 06, which meant a mix of Navy captains and a few Marine Corps colonels. Each family would live in this ideal setting for two to three years at best and then move on. They were pleasant and neighborly. But all the couples, except for Pam and Randolph were white. Most days it didn't make a difference. Rank seemed to sometimes trump race within the military.

Pam and Randolph dined regularly with most of their neighbors because the active duty person in each of those houses had a common mission. They worked together in varying capacities and considered themselves a part of a team. This camaraderie carried over to their spouses, and it seemed they all had spouses. A single senior officer living in military housing was a rare bird indeed. During this tour, there were no senior active duty women living on Captain's Row with civilian husbands. It was assumed and somewhat required that your spouse uproot her life when you received your orders. Thus, most of the wives didn't work outside the home at that point in their husbands' careers. As long as you stayed away from politics, religion and race; everybody seemed to get along fine.

Pam had one dear friend on Porter Road: Anne Devereux McDonald. Anne and Pam had been best friends since their husbands were midshipmen at the Naval Academy. Randolph and Jackson were in the same company and were both on the sailing team. Anne and Jackson had only one son, Lieutenant Jackson McDonald Jr., and Anne thought of Pam's girls as her own. Theirs was a comfortable friendship with longevity. Anne was a fearless blonde from New Orleans who stood almost 6 feet. They were sisters of the south and shared a common bond of overcoming crappy childhoods. Living on the yard, Pam and Anne worked on two committees together with the Naval Officers' Wives Club and had lunch together every Thursday.

Pam and Anne could and did talk about everything. They'd been stationed together four times and when they weren't in the same city they talked on the phone and often vacationed together. Pam and Anne were godparents to each other's children, Jack Jr. and Rachel. They were pregnant together in Pascagoula, Mississippi, while Randolph and Jackson were stationed on a pre-commissioned ship being built there. It was the only time Pam had been stationed in her hometown.

Even though they met through their husbands when they were both newly married, over the years they'd grown closer and their friendship moved beyond the fine foursome the two couples made. They knew each other's secrets, strengths and weaknesses and more importantly, where the bones were buried.

Living in the mansions on the campus of the Naval Academy was commonly called living "on the yard." It was convenient to walk to everything and the weekly parades, lectures and the shot in the arm of just being around so many young optimistic college students, made life pleasant. Everyone had a place. Everyone knew their place and everyone kept pace…for the most part.

Chapter 2

....

The door was unlocked and she walked into the foyer trying not to make too much noise on the shiny hardwood floors. Tipping onto the deep blue Oriental rug, Pam slid her shoes off and placed them neatly into the basket by the door. The first floor of the house had a living room and a massive dining room, both with lovely brick fireplaces. There was also a large butler's pantry, a powder room, and a huge eat-in kitchen with lots of natural light.

The dining room even had a patched up wooden circle on the floor near the chair closest to the kitchen. This was where the call button was once nestled against the floorboards. The lady of the house would discreetly step on the button and a buzzer would sound in both the kitchen and butler's pantry to alert the maids and cook when help was needed to clear the table and bring in another course. It brought Pam some secret joy that only one having been oppressed could understand, when she thought of how all those maids, butlers and cooks looked like her. They were black and that was their lot in life. The expectation was that they would remain a part of the serving class. Now she was the lady of the house. Yes, her black self was the lady of the house and she felt she had somehow avenged them or made their struggle worth something. She hoped their spirits were happy with their connected journeys.

All of the furniture on the first floor was period furniture, mostly antiques on loan from the Naval Academy storehouse. The dark mahogany curved wood pieces all fit perfectly with the 100-year old house. The couches and chairs were various shades of beige and cream. The throw pillows, table linens and dishes were blue and red. It was patriotic. Pam and Randolph had the furniture that actually belonged to them on the second and third floors of the quarters. Each floor had three large bedrooms and two bathrooms.

There was even a basement. It was dark with exposed brick walls and pipes in the ceiling. Some said that all the basements used to house rows of twin-sized beds and were used as servants' quarters. Pam didn't know. She hadn't bothered to research it. For her, the most glorious thing about the house on Porter Road was the screened-in wraparound porch with its blue and white striped awnings. She loved porches and had since she was a girl in Mississippi. Some of her fondest memories, the good ones, were of the times she, Daddy Sloane and her sister Ella Jean. They sat on the front porch surrounded by twinkling fireflies drinking homemade lemonade out of mason jars. She spent a lot of time on this porch at 7 Porter Road. It was a peaceful place for her.

Pam tiptoed towards the massive French doors leading to her sanctuary. Opening the door and slipping through, she made her way to her favorite of the four white wicker chaises on the porch and sat down. After texting Randolph "*I'm home, come stop the crazy,*" she put the phone down on the wicker table next to her, beside a round vase hugging pale blue hydrangeas. Resting both feet on the wicker ottoman, she leaned back and closed her eyes.

Randolph was in his office when the phone beeped with her message. He continued to type on his desktop vowing to get the speech he was giving for the National Naval Officers Association program next week written before putting his favorite daughter's hand into her new husband, Jared's hand.

René had always been his favorite. He denied it but she knew it and so did the other girls. He loved them all and they were all by and large Daddy's girls. But René, the third of four had been born when he was deployed. He missed her birth and perhaps it was that guilt that bound them together or just the fact that both of them had to work so hard to "learn" each other when he returned home to a 5 month old in the throes of separation anxiety. She cried every time he looked at her and slowly over time she came to understand that he was "Daddy" and by the time she was three they were inseparable. She was his road dog. As she grew up, she was interested in everything dad was interested in. René liked numbers; she played golf with him and was logical and reserved – like Randolph. He didn't have to work hard to understand her and that suited him fine.

Randolph glanced at the phone, annoyed that Pam didn't come upstairs to talk to him but texted instead. He typed lightly, "*on my way down*." He put the speech away. It was almost completed anyway. He'd finish the rest later. Pushing the comfortable navy blue leather chair away from the desk and straightening the small stack of folders on top of the desk for the fourth time, he prepared to go down three flights of stairs to his wife. To calm Pam and execute the day with precision and without incident was his objective. He was prepared to do whatever it took.

Her husband's presence was signaled by darkness permeating Pam's closed lids because he blocked her light. She hadn't heard him step out onto the porch. Opening her eyes, she took him in. Every time she saw him, she felt the same - happy, centered and at peace. It had been almost 31 years and a lot had changed, but that remained the same. She loved him and they were friends.

Randolph slid beside her in his khakis, pink polo shirt and plain brown loafers. He wasn't wearing socks and he never wore jewelry, just a watch and his wedding band. His strong brown hand reached for hers and they just sat in silence for a while. Each at peace with the life they'd built. Regardless of how the day went and how the wedding went, they both knew they'd gotten that part right. They loved each other and their love had incubated and nurtured their four girls. They felt it and from it, felt armed to take on the world and its challenges.

Chapter 3

....

The peaceful silence was broken by soft singing growing louder as the sound approached the porch. The doors opened and their youngest daughter, Rae continued to sing, "Going to the chapel and I'm gonna get married....going to the chapel of love..." Rae plopped down across from them and hummed a little of her tune before mischievously taunting her parents.

"Top of the morning to you, Captain and Mrs. Hamilton, you some good-looking colored folk."

Pam rolled her eyes and Randolph smiled.

"Good morning, Miss Rae. Thank you for the compliment, did you sleep well?"

"Like a baby, daddy. Like a baby."

Pam chuckled, "That's because you are a baby." She turned to Randolph and winked. "Honey, isn't nineteen still a baby?"

"I do believe so." Randolph joined in the teasing.
"I am a junior in college and I have my own apartment and my own car. I ain't no baby!"

Pam frowned, "Not ain't Rae."

"Oh mom, I speak correct English, I'm on the dean's list for the sixth semester in a row. I was just code switching. We all do it on some level." Rae was serious.

"Okay, this is not the day for sociological, philosophical or theological discourse. I already have a headache and it's not even nine o'clock."

"It's because you drink too much champagne and you eat red meat," Rae exclaimed, loudly.

"Girl, you are not my mama. I am yours. How's that for code switching?"

Rae laughed and started in on her favorite subject of late, the groom-to-be: Jared Foster Reed.

"So do you really think his parents aren't coming because they're missionaries and can't get away from the mission fields?" Rae quizzed, smirking.

Randolph shifted in his seat signaling his discomfort with the subject. He hated gossip or speaking negatively of people. No matter what, he just didn't do it. Rae, on the hand was a 19-year-old super sleuth. The youngest of the four girls, she entertained herself with her sisters' business with regularity. Growing up it was her favorite pastime.

"Y'all know good and well, that boy's parents ain't nobody's missionaries. You can find anyone with a Google search, but not them. Jared's parents, the holy missionaries seemed to have vanished into thin air without a trace. And if he had spent his early childhood on foreign missions, raised by devout Christians wouldn't he halfway like God or know some biblical stuff? That boy doesn't even know the words to the basic hymns. I bet even the devil knows the words to 'Amazing Grace.' He only pretends to like church and he's probably pretending about a whole lot of other stuff too."

Pam rubbed her head as the headache was returning with even greater intensity than before. Randolph furrowed his brow and squinted, shifting a bit in his chair again. He opened his mouth to speak but before he could steer his daughter off the course she was on, Rae spoke.

Chiding them both on the edge of her chair she pointed.

"Riddle me that, oh wonderful, comfortable, colored parents? Riddle me that?"

"Stop talking like that Rae, it isn't nice. Jared has nothing to prove to anyone. The Navy does a thorough background check and if there were any areas of concern he would not have the level of security clearance he has," Randolph spoke, firmly directing a disapproving gaze at his youngest daughter.

Chapter 4

....

Rae jumped up from the edge of the pale yellow and soft blue floral splattered settee she had been perched on and began pacing the cool tan wooden floor in her bare feet. Her skinny jeans and gray t-shirt camouflaging both age and gender, Rae could easily pass for a 16-year-old boy. She stood five feet and weighed 100 pounds soaking wet. Her hair was cut short and naturally curly; her most recent act of defining herself was to dye it copper. With the most childlike sand colored face and large expressive golden brown eyes, she was gorgeous. The beauty of it was she either didn't know it or didn't care. She spent little time with what she called the foolishness of primping, wore no makeup and dressed for comfort. She was funny and quick, both mentally and physically.

"Stop calling us colored! That's not cute, Rae." Pam's eyes were fixed on her pacing daughter.

She grimaced at this new *"code switching" let me sound like an ignorant uncultured fool because by Daddy drives a Mercedes and has several college degrees, foolishness.* Pam was fed up with her daughter and other young kids who had the luxury of going back and forth because they knew how to communicate effectively. Pam didn't grow up with that luxury and had to work hard to learn correct grammar, diction and speech. Last night at the rehearsal dinner, her oldest daughter, Rachel explained this new phenomenon as the ease with which most minorities move from one method of expression to another. She said it was a good thing.

Pam wasn't sure. All she knew was that she paid good money for a top-rated education in private schools and helped with homework every night for too many years for this child to sound like "Dumb Debbie."

"Well, if Jared says his parents are missionaries then we ought to take him at his word. He will be family in just a few hours, Rae." Pam sounded as if she was trying to convince herself that he would indeed be family by nightfall. She could hear Anne's voice in her head from last Thursday's lunch at Agua Terra. Anne was suspicious of Jared from the first time they met. She had warned Pam to watch him but not to speak against him. Her theory was that the bond between Jared and René would be strengthened if they had a common foe.

She'd joked, "Before I met Jackson, I collected creeps for a hobby. I am an expert on creeps and something is not right about Jared. He has a lot of characteristics commonly found in creeps."

Pam had not become one of the common foes that would strengthen their bond. But her daughters were united in their dislike and distrust of Jared. No one was as vocal as Rae, but René knew how each of them felt. Perhaps the conservative military world René and Jared lived in with its subtle prejudices concerning interracial marriage had pushed them closer together too. It didn't matter. None of it mattered to Pam. They were getting married today. Nothing was going to stop that. If René loved this man, they were going to make it work.

Last week, Anne had giggled as she went through her list of collected creeps in great detail. Pam listened and laughed, shrugging it off, but now on the day of the wedding she was feeling a little worried. She would just not show it and she would put this behind her. René loved Jared and Jared said he loved her and that was all there was to it.

Her thoughts were interrupted by Rae.

"You know what? His parents are probably in jail or dead because he killed them," Rae grinned, excitedly.

"Okay, that's enough; don't you have some things to do this morning?" Randolph stood signaling the end of this discussion for him and moved toward the door to return to his study.

"I'll be upstairs if you ladies need me."

As soon as the door closed behind her dad, Rae sat down next to her mother, leaning in close, staring at her face for clues that she too was suspicious of Jared.

"Do you really think René loves him and wants to marry him? Why is she doing this? Why is she marrying this white guy nobody knows? What happened to Tony?" She waited searching her mother's face for some great revelation.

"René is in love. What's done is done, the train has left the station and there is nothing any of us can do. Tony may have been your choice baby, but he wasn't hers. It's been three years since they broke up, let it go. Behave today. No snooping and no crazy."

"Oh, I'm bringing some crazy!" Rae laughed from her gut and bounced off the cushion jumping as she stood.

"I've got to get ready to go to see what my crew is doing. Rachel and Reagan said we'd have breakfast with René before she jumps the broom with 'the ice man' and I don't mean Jerry Butler."

Rae's voice trailed off as she left the room. She mumbled a barely audible, "I'll be watching him."

Chapter 5

….

The girls and their husbands, Trent and Sean, stayed at the house with Pam and Randolph while Jared stayed at his townhouse off of West Street. René's things were scheduled to arrive from her Manhattan apartment after the honeymoon. Pam was excited to have her daughter living in Annapolis near her. Reagan, Rachel and Rae all lived in the D.C. area so this would mean more opportunities to do things together.

Jared had not come to the house last night after the rehearsal dinner but instead declared he was tired, had a few whispered words with his bride-to-be and said goodnight. He seemed to be more distant lately. You would think he'd be feeling closer to René's family. But he seemed to stay away more often and especially this wedding weekend. He was grown and he could stay wherever he wanted but he wasn't making it easier to become a part of the family by segregating himself.

Pam felt a familiar sensation. The hot flashes and the dry mouth seemed to proceed the hammering in her head. She went to search for relief before the onslaught of her daughters and the wedding. In the kitchen she moved her green wooden step stool over to the cabinet and reached up to the mint green covered dish with pretty, pink flowers. Looking around to make sure she was alone, she pulled the small bowl off the shelf and stepped down from the stool. Feet planted firmly on the floor, Pam lifted the delicate porcelain lid with routine quietness. This was one of three stashes. She selected one small pill and placed the lid back on the dish and climbed back on the stool balancing her relief in both hands. Pushing it back on the top shelf in the far corner she closed the cabinet door and stepped down. Grabbing a small glass she ran the tap water and swallowed the Percocet. The pain would be gone soon.

Pam had never intended to take pain medicine so often and she didn't take it every day. She told herself this was not an addiction because of that one fact. The problem was that the Tylenol and the over the counter stuff just did nothing but eat at her stomach. The pain was still there.

"If I'm not in pain, then I don't know who is? Isn't that what pain medication is for, to relieve pain?" She justified taking the stashed pills out loud, spilling denial in to the empty room.

She was not abusing prescription drugs and in her mind she simply was not the kind of person who did. All she wanted was to feel better and nobody needed to know. Randolph would be furious. He just wouldn't understand. He thought Nyquil was a deadly drug. He took nothing and was as healthy and fit as he'd been when they met thirty-five years ago. He was still the same Eagle Scout he'd been at eighteen. She didn't know him then but when she met the young, handsome midshipman 2nd class at twenty, there was something so irresistibly honest and pure about him. He calmed her in every way. Pam knew he wouldn't understand her taking these pills. So she didn't tell him. But the headaches came more often now and especially after the dreams. The horrible dreams wouldn't stop. There would be a whole week or maybe a few weeks and things were fine. Then out of nowhere the dreams returned. It was always the same hauntingly strange dream.

The room was almost dark except for a lone candle blazing with white light. It stood on the only bare space on the cold floor beside a little girl who sat naked in a lonely basement. The floor was a blanket of dead birds that silently threatened the child's sanity. Blood poured as if flowing from a faucet from both her eyes and ears. She was covered in filth and wept as the screaming hawks, crows, bats, vultures and buzzards circled above her. Pam could never make out the little girl's face. There was so much blood and so many shadows, voices and the bleeding eyes and ears. Every time the largest vulture got close enough to touch the girl...

Pam woke up.

The dreams came from nowhere and caused her resist sleep. The lack of sleep made her irritable and contributed to the headaches. So this was the treadmill she'd been on for a little over a year now. She made a promise that after the wedding she would stop taking pain meds and start taking better care of herself. Yes, she would put all of this to rest. Things would calm down and get back to normal. She just wanted some peace.

She hadn't thought about her mother in a long time. She worked hard to keep thoughts of Jean out of her conscious mind.

"I didn't have a good mother but I am going to be one or die trying," she mumbled under her breath.

With that she took a deep sigh and pushed the past out of her mind. Believing that God could and did answer prayer, she prayed at the foot of the long winding mahogany staircase.

"Get me through this day. Help me to give my girls the support and wisdom they need. Help me to reflect you, Lord. Get me through it...in Jesus' name. Amen."

Chapter 6

....

As Pam paused in the foyer admiring the beautiful navy blue Oriental rug on the gleaming hardwood floors and the antique brass sconces flanking the massive oval mirror, she heard the voices of her daughters. Putting her game face on, she slowly climbed the stairs. The girls were on the second floor of the three-story house. This floor housed the master bedroom and two guest rooms currently used by Rachel and Reagan and their husbands, Trent and Sean. Rae and René where on the third floor where there were two rooms used for sleeping and one for Randolph's office. She heard no male voices and assumed the guys were not up yet. Approaching the landing, Pam saw her daughters.

Rachel, the oldest of the four flashed the warmest smile and was the first to greet her. She was the color of café con leche with her black hair still wrapped around her head and pinned neatly in strategic spots. Wearing pale pink slippers with a pink satin robe clinging to her small frame, she grinned. Her driving forces were support and kindness.

"Good morning, Mom. How's everything going?" Reagan, her middle daughter chimed in before Pam could answer. Reagan was a jazz artist and a visiting professor at Howard University. She was tall and sultry exuding confidence and sensuality. A true bohemian, Reagan was the most casual of the four sisters.

"Hey Mom, today is the big day! It's on now! René's got jungle fever!"

Pam kissed her two married daughters while Rae stood grinning at Reagan's "jungle fever" comment. The girls were heading upstairs to see if René was up so they could help her get ready.

"Listen, we are not going to do this. We are not prejudiced. We believe that people are people. All people have value and we are not going to let Jared's race become an issue. I won't have it."

Pam spoke in a soft serious tone. All three girls looked at her with mock seriousness that exploded into laughter. Rachel tried to explain what they were really feeling.

"Oh Mom, we're not prejudiced either. But I guess when you know something is wrong and you can't name it you go after the thing you can name. Jared is creepy and I don't - we don't - like who René becomes when she's with him. She checks her brain at the door and seems distant. So we tease about him being white, but that's a front. Rae dated Vic from Spain last year we loved every white inch of him. My godparents, Annie D. and Jack Mac are white. So this is not about race. It's something else, and we're just being foolish. I guess it's a kind of laughing to keep from crying thing. I'm sorry Mom. We don't want to cause drama."

Reagan and Rae looked helpless but said nothing.

"Go on down to the kitchen, get some coffee started and make the batter for the waffles, I'll check in on René."

The trio headed downstairs as Pam walked up the third and final flight of stairs towards the bride's door.

Chapter 7

….

Knocking lightly and then letting herself in, she found her daughter sitting in the middle of her bed amidst a sea of butter yellow pillows, sheets and comforters. The room had no patterns on the wall or on the linen. The walls were the same buttery yellow color as the comforter and pillows and the room was in the front of the house. It was Pam's favorite room, with the antique mahogany four poster rice bed and two comfortable pale yellow club chairs sitting against the wall. The only picture was a framed reproduction of Van Gogh's "Yellow Sunflowers."

The room was huge but warm and René was awake and frowning. She looked tiny sitting in the middle of the soft yellow sea with wild curly hair that draped her thin milk chocolate shoulders. René looked calm but disappointed. The sadness on her face went beyond overhearing her sisters berate Jared. There was something else, and a whole lot of it too.

"Mom, do you think the walls and doors are sound proof?" She quipped before Pam could answer.

"Well, they're not. I can hear you guys. I can always hear you. I hear you in my sleep and it hurts. I love him."

Pam sat down next to her daughter and drew her close.

"Honey, I know and I'm sorry. Your sisters just want you to be happy. I know you think they're being mean. But I know that is not their intention. I'm on your side and I know they are too. Always remember that. People can do some really stupid things trying to protect someone they love. I promise you it will get better. They will get to know Jared better and love him. You know when you all get together things get bigger than life. They just get this little mob mentality going and they egg each other on, seeing who can be the silliest. They love you and they will learn to love Jared."

She let go of René and really looked at her sad face, a face too sad to be a wedding day face. There was so much determination. When she spoke of Jared, Pam heard determination, not love.

"René, I like Jared. We just know so little about him. He's in the Navy and he was an aide for Admiral Braxton, but we don't know his family. That's all. Knowing someone's people helps you to know them so much better, and we have none of that and you've dated for two whole years. Besides, twenty-three is so young to be getting married."

René shook her head impatiently.

"Mom, you were twenty-three when you and Dad got married, don't be such a hypocrite."

"That was a hundred years ago! We didn't know any better. Everybody got married right after college in the stone ages."

Pam laughed and it brought a reluctant smile to René's face.

"Get dressed and let's meet downstairs. You are going to be a beautiful bride, but you have to eat something, even if it's just some fruit. It's going to be a wonderful day, but it's going to be a long one."

Pam got up from the bed and smoothed the wrinkles from her linen dress. She turned towards the door and then turned back.

"Hey kiddo, let's pray. My daddy prayed with me on my wedding day and it calmed my nerves so much."

René didn't move from the middle of the bed, but she reached both of her arms out towards Pam, signaling her willingness to pray. Pam took René's hands in both of hers and stood as they both bowed their heads and closed their eyes in the familiar ritual. Pam began to speak softly.

"Father God, thank you for this beautiful woman before me. Thank you for keeping her safe as a child and wrapping your arm of protection around her today and tomorrow. We ask your blessings and your undergirding of this union. Let them be happy, Lord and let today be flawless and let them both keep you in the center of their lives and remain in the center of your will. These and all other prayers we ask in Jesus' name. Amen"

They opened their eyes and Pam felt better somehow. René, on the other hand thought about the fact that Jared didn't believe in God or organized religion. She wondered if her parents knew he was faking when he eagerly attended the base chapel with them as if it were something he enjoyed doing. She wondered if they knew his soft "amens" during the worship service were just lip service. She didn't care. She loved him and he would change. He just needed time and he needed to feel like he belonged to someone. She was prepared to be his sanctuary. René felt she had enough faith to sustain them both.

Pam's phone rang and she pulled it from her pocket. Shayla, the wedding planner, was on the other end assuring her that the cake had arrived and everything was on schedule. She sounded confident and triumphant. Pam sighed with relief and terminated the call, heading out the door to gather everyone for today's big event. They were going to have a wedding, no matter what.

Her head had finally stopped hurting and the Percocet was in full effect. She didn't take them often and even though Randolph didn't know, Anne knew. Pam had gotten the prescription when she had a hysterectomy two years ago and between the two of them they had managed to invent enough mysterious pains to get more from the clinic. Pam liked the way life was a little blurred around the edges when she took the pills. They helped her to forget the god-awful nightmares she had been having. But her speech never slurred and she was never anything short of herself in public.

Chapter 8

….

Two doors on the second floor opened and closed quietly.   Trent sat up when he heard his wife come in.

"Good morning babe, are you ready for this crazy wedding?" Rachel kissed his lips gently. Trent pulled her close to his 6′ 2″ frame sitting at the desk and moved his laptop back and sat Rachel on top of the desk.

"When my butt types new numbers on your report, don't be mad at me, be mad at yourself and my big butt."

"I'm sure that anything your round and proud bottom chooses to add will be an improvement to the document." He stroked her bare brown legs and kissed her deeply.

"So did you take the test this morning, Rache?"

Rachel hopped off the desk with quickness.

"No, Trent, I didn't take the pregnancy test yet."

"You know it's supposed to be the first urine to get the truest reading." Trent looked directly at his wife standing in front of him in her silk pink pajamas, no shoes and hands defiantly on her hips.

"Trent, I didn't pee yet, okay? This can't be all you talk about with me! For the past year it has consumed us. I won't let it, Trent, I won't."

Her voice trailed off as she went into the adjoining bathroom and closed the door.

Trent knew she was lying. He'd heard her in the bathroom before she joined her sisters and Pam in the hallway. He sat at the desk staring at the pictures of young Rachel on the tennis team, as a cheerleader and prom queen that lined the walls. She was beautiful, always had been. Marrying her 6 years ago had been the smartest move he'd made. His friends jokingly called it his "key acquisition." She'd been his friend through college and law school. They'd been through the death of his father and suing his law firm. This baby thing was not going to break them. It was just another hurdle to clear and they'd cleared too many to lose. But ever since they were both cleared by their doctors of any physical infertility issues, things had been tense. Sex wasn't even fun anymore. It had become a job, a duty for both of them. Neither of them said a word but they both felt it.

Rachel ran water into the porcelain sink and sat on the toilet with the lid closed. She looked at the color of the toenail polish on her bare feet on the cold tile. They felt good. The pale pink matched the delicate pattern of pastels in the wallpaper. The soft pink towels spoke to her mother's sense of style. Pam always made things look prettier than they really were. She knew her time was running out so she flushed the toilet to make Trent think she'd actually peed. She grabbed one of the dozen or so home pregnancy kit tubes from her overnight bag and tore it open, tossing the wrapping in the sink. Running hot water over it while she watched the indicators become saturated made her feel like a sorry cheat. But she was exhausted.

They had tried everything and she was just beginning to think they needed to look into adoption or surrogacy. Maybe Reagan would carry their child. She had those big baby making hips. Free love, free thinking, Reagan had no problem whatsoever getting pregnant. But that was before she got married. Thinking about her sister made her smile but the smile left as quickly as it had come because the sound of the soft tapping on the door brought her back to her sorry situation. Trent's knock was predictable.

"Rachel, can I come in?"

She moved slowly, lifting the lid without a sound. Rachel slid her underwear and pajama pants down her legs and watched them pool around her feet. Stepping out and leaving them in a heap of regret on the floor, she opened the door and sat back down on the toilet seat. Trent entered quietly and looked at her with so much love and tenderness. He looked at her hands expectedly for the test and positive results. The test stick rested in the bottom of bathroom sink. She pointed. It was official, she knew she had to be the most evil and deceptive person in the world.

There was probably a special corner of hell twenty degrees hotter for people who lied to their husband's about stuff like this.

"No luck this time. No baby for us," Rachel murmured looking down at her pink toenails.

Trent lifted her chin and kissed her sweaty forehead.

"It's fine. We'll keep trying and praying. It'll happen."

"Trent. Can we just give it a break? Having a baby is not like passing the bar. It's not some career aspiration like making partner. We don't have to prove anything to anybody. What's the rush?" She finally got the words out that she'd been choking on for months. Trent saw what he thought was fear in his wife's eyes.

"What's wrong, Rache, you don't feel ready?" He felt completely surprised by her questions and the silence that ensued.

"No. I think there are so many things I want to do before I become a mother. There. I said it."

"It's fine, you should have told me how you felt. I'm sorry too. It's fine. We're fine." Trent spoke in an effort to convince both he and his wife. They got dressed in silence and headed downstairs to catch whatever else the day was throwing their way.

Chapter 9

....

In the room next door, Sean lay naked in the bed with the soft silk sheets draped around his waist exposing his chiseled chest. Both he and Reagan were gym rats and it showed. As Reagan entered the room, he closed his eyes. Reagan pulled the oversized t-shirt she'd stolen from Sean years ago over her head, exposing her naked slender body. The gray worn "Revenge of the Nerds" t-shirt lay crumpled on the floor as she lifted the covers and pressed her body against Sean's. He reached for her and wrapped his arms around her gently moving on top of her. Their lips and bodies met with the urgency of desire and pleasure that was all their own. Their bodies communicated their silent passion and no words were spoken. And then it was over.

Sean fell onto the bed positioning his body next to his wife listening to her breathing heavily.

"Thank you."

She closed her eyes and stroked her husband's chest. Her long legs wrapped around his thigh.

"You seem tired and you feel thin, honey. Is everything okay?" Sean pulled her in closer. It hurt.

"I'm fine Sean, stop worrying." Reagan tried to loosen his grip by inching slightly away from his warm body.

"Okay, take your vitamins, Reagan. I'd like to keep you for the long haul." Sean pulled away and got up to go shower.

"Yeah, I plan to be here for the long haul. I've trained you now and it took me four years to do it. Yep, I'm staying. It's gonna be 'til death do us part. Hope I don't have to kill you!" Reagan laughed loudly at her own joke as the bathroom door closed.

He was right, she'd lost ten pounds. Sean was so in tune to her, her body, her needs. She loved him and she rested in bed thinking what a good guy he was and how he didn't deserve such a liar for a wife. Reagan had her third miscarriage last month while Sean was away at the National Black Accountants Regional Conference. He was excited about being one of the presenters and she didn't want to call and tell him she was bleeding again.

She called Rachel instead and made her promise not to tell Pam. With all the tension surrounding the wedding she didn't want to add more negative energy. That night it rained and Rachel came, bottle of merlot in hand and sat with her sister as they each lamented their own "baby blues." Rachel went on about how much Trent wanted a baby and how sick she was of having mechanical sex just to procreate. She compared it to having a part-time job. Reagan talked about karma and reaping what you sow, she had two abortions while in Paris on tour. This was long before she knew she wanted Sean. He'd been just a friend for so many years. She was young and single and having fun and she just couldn't have a baby out of wedlock and be Pam and Randolph's daughter. She knew she couldn't tell her bible toting mother that she'd had an abortion. Sean didn't even know about the abortions before they were married or the last two pregnancies and subsequent miscarriages. Rachel was her only confidante and she promised not to tell anyone, ever. Reagan was sure God was punishing her.

That night in her condo living room she sat on the floor propped up against her bright orange couch and listened. Her big sister and best friend, Rachel assured her that God was not capricious and wouldn't be punishing her for the sins of her past with miscarriages.

"Damn, Reagan. What kind of God do you serve? God is not the boogie man or some scary monster. He has forgiven you. Those abortions were over five years ago. You asked for forgiveness, didn't you?" Rachel spoke in soothing tones as her sister sobbed.

"Yes, you know I did. But God is pointing at me right now and laughing." Reagan spoke blowing her nose into a wad of brightly colored cocktail napkins.

"God is saying, 'this is what you get you little slut puppy! So you wanna baby now but when you were sleeping with those French men you weren't thinking about a baby. You didn't want a baby then, ho. Boom!'"

They both burst into uncontrollable laughter, Rachel spilling her deep red wine onto the kidney shaped glass coffee table. Tears continued to trail Reagan's face.

"You are a fool, Reagan, a pure fool!" She screamed with laughter as she ran into the kitchen to get a towel to clean the table. Reagan moved the four art books to the floor to avoid the wine spill and chuckled.

"First thing, God does not speak slang! Second thing, God does not use derogatory names. Come on Reagan, really. *Slut puppy?* Third thing, Reagan, is that the risen triumphant Savior of the universe does not call people whores or hoes and HE doesn't taunt us! And the final thing, baby, is that I don't think God uses 'Boom' to punctuate his points! I think he's a bit more formal."

They were both crying and laughing at this point. Still laughing, Rachel cleaned the table with the dish towel and went back into the kitchen to rinse it out so the wine wouldn't leave permanent stains. Returning to her sister's modern and colorful living room Rachel marveled at her crazy sister, Reagan, legs formed into a pretzel, still laughing and crying.

Rachel scolded her sister.

"Reagan, your God sounds an awful lot like you. The gospel according to Reagan is not the gospel according to anybody's bible and thank God for that. Your God sounds scary, judgmental and mean. I wouldn't want to tangle with the likes of him!"

She knelt on the floor beside Reagan who was younger but the taller of the two. Rachel wrapped both of her bony arms around her and squeezed inhaling her sister's expensive perfume. They sat like that in silence for a while, both of them hoping not to disappoint their parents, husbands and younger sisters. They needed to be the picture of success that everybody thought was their destiny. It continued to rain until late into the night.

Reagan was brought back to the here and now by her husband's beautiful naked body. Sean came out of the bathroom dripping wet with his towel around his neck. Sitting up in the bed to take in the full show, Reagan said,

"A lot of good that towel is doing." He laughed and stood in front of her drying himself.

"Come on, lazy bones, let's get this party started."

Per his request, Reagan got herself into the bathroom to shower and get downstairs to breakfast. She made a silent vow not to think about the rainy sad night with Rachel after the most recent devastating loss. Today she decided not to think about the five babies she did not have.

Chapter 10

....

The Naval Academy Chapel was beautiful. Pam felt relaxed and calm in a sea of white uniforms. Trent and Sean looked quite handsome in their tuxedos as they stood in front of the church alongside three of Jared's friends. Dr Tony Green, who briefly dated René when she was in college, was Jared's only close friend and stood flanked by the two ensigns Paul and Frank who worked for Jared. They were fillers there to walk with René's two best friends, Stacy and Kayla. They didn't like Jared, they feared him. They had seen him ruin too many careers, so if he said they were in his wedding then they were in his wedding.

Tony just didn't like that he lost René and tried to put the whole thing behind him. He wasn't cheating. He'd gone out a couple of times with her cousin when she first moved to Atlanta and wanted help making decisions about med school. He'd only done it as a favor to René's mom, Pam, who was like his aunt. They had been out about four times, a couple of lunches and dinners. There had been nothing more than that. Period. He thought René had been unreasonable and unfair when she accused him of cheating with Michelle. So when he found out Jared was dating René, he said nothing other than that he knew their family well. Their mothers had come from the same small town in Mississippi.

Pam sat next to Randolph, who was lost in his own thoughts. He believed they all needed to give Jared a chance. Randolph liked him. Pam's half-sister Ella Jean sat next to her and next to Ella Jean was her daughter, Michelle. Ella Jean was four years older than Pam and was their crazy mother's love child. No one knew who her father was, not even Ella

Jean. Daddy Sloane had loved both Ella Jean and Pam as if they were both his own even though Pam was his only child. Next to Michelle and Ella Jean were Anne and Jackson and then Randolph's parents and his brother and his wife and their two teenage kids. The rest of the pews were filled with relatives and countless civilian and military friends made along the way. The church looked like the United Nations.

Ella Jean sat proudly between her baby sister and her daughter, Michelle. These were the two people she loved most. Both had saved her by coming into the world. Although she was only four when her mother got pregnant with Pam, her whole life changed. Finally there was food in the refrigerator and not just beer for her mother's boyfriends. Her mother, Jean, was home more often. Jean almost never left the house and Daddy Sloane, her newest boyfriend and the baby's father, married her. She was now somebody's wife. She was respectable. Before the marriage, Ella Jean was with her sick grandmother or home by herself a lot of the time. She was hungry and scared and spent all of her energy trying not to anger Jean. Jean drank Jack Daniels and once joked, that "ole Jack" was her one true love. To this day, Ella Jean hated the smell of liquor. Getting slapped in the face for calling her mother "mama" instead of Jean or some other seemingly insignificant infraction was as much a part of her daily routine as waking up.

When Pam was born and Jean married, the beatings stopped. Ella Jean even allowed her daughters to call her mama instead of Jean. Although by then Ella Jean didn't want to call her mama. She had settled into the relationship and its parameters. She avoided calling Jean, mother and more importantly feeling anything for her negative or positive. She tried to never be alone with her now that there were other people in their house all the time; she felt protected.

Chapter 11

….

They moved in with Daddy Sloane and his house was clean with three bedrooms and a small yard. It was one of a few brick houses in the black section of town. But the best thing was the food. There was so much food. Daddy Sloane did all the cooking and he'd make big juicy hams and meatloaf and sweet potatoes and everything. Ella Jean ate and ate, as if trying to make up for all the days and nights she existed on grits.

Her mother Jean would make a pot of grits about twice a week and leave it on the stove. When it was first cooked and if they had margarine in the refrigerator, that was good. Ella Jean was not allowed to use sugar in the grits because it was Jean's and reserved for her coffee. She tried once and still has the burn on her wrist from the lesson she was taught about disobeying Jean or "messin' with her stuff." By lunch time, the pot of grits was stiff and pasty, but if she was hungry, she had to push the chair to the stove, climb up on it while balancing her bowl and use the huge wooden spoon to serve herself lunch. The same dance was repeated without music at dinner time. By then the grits were ice cold and it didn't matter if they had margarine or not. It would sit on the top of the cold white cereal with defiant stubbornness. Ella Jean was four and couldn't manage to put the heavy pot in the refrigerator and Jean didn't care to. So the second and third day the grits were sour and sticky. She ate them anyway and often vomited and had diarrhea that she had to clean up with her own little four-year old hands.

By the time Daddy Sloane came into the picture, Ella Jean was no longer bothered by her mother spending her days in her bed watching TV. She was happy and relieved that Jean completely ignored her because that was far better than being the single focus of all of her bad moods and anger. She welcomed the neglect like her closest friend. So Daddy Sloane's visits changed everything. Jean was dressed more often and the three of them went for rides in Daddy Sloane's truck on Sunday's. Jean even stopped cussing at her and seemed almost happy.

Ella Jean could tell that her mother wanted Daddy Sloane to think she was a good person and a good mother. But the sad thing for him was that by the time he realized she was neither a good mother nor a good person, she was pregnant with his child, Pam. He was not a careless man and he had gotten to be thirty years old without any illegitimate babies. Jean said she couldn't have "no more babies" and like a fool, he believed her. So they got married because in those days that was what decent men and women did. Knowing that Jean was mean, selfish and incapable of love didn't stop her new husband from loving her. He accepted her on her terms and loved the parts she allowed him to love.

When Ella Jean was six, she and Daddy Sloane took care of two-year old Pam completely. They had settled into a routine and become a family. Jean slept a lot, talked on the phone and watched her stories on TV. Daddy Sloane made sure the clothes were clean and the house was too. He made breakfast each day after getting the girls up from the room they shared with the double bed they both slept in. He got them washed and dressed and took Pam to Miss Freddy's to be looked after until his work day was over and dropped Ella Jean off at Robert E. Lee elementary school. Each morning they'd sit in the small white kitchen at the green table with four vinyl backed chairs with silver metal legs. The fourth chair was almost always empty because Jean took her meals in her bedroom on a tray that Daddy Sloane brought her if she was awake. If she wasn't, then before leaving for work he'd fill a tin pie pan with cheese eggs, sausage, grits and biscuits and cover it in foil and place it on top of the stove on a pot of hot water for his wife to eat whenever she woke up. Taking care of Pam and having Daddy Sloane to take care of her was the first joy Ella Jean had known.

Chapter 12

....

Ella Jean looked over at her beautiful, successful, daughter sitting on the pew right next to her. Their legs were close enough to touch. Michelle smelled like prosperity and completeness to Ella Jean. This wedding was Pam's third and Ella Jean knew that one day soon, Michelle would find and settle down with the right man. She had made great sacrifices and as the organist played she couldn't help but count the cost and remember how far they both had come.

When Michelle was born, Ella Jean was at her lowest point. She had to come home from college disgraced. She dropped out of school and everybody in Pascagoula, Mississippi was whispering about the father's identity. She'd thought about getting rid of the baby. It had almost happened. Ella Jean shivered a little on her pew thinking about what her life would have been without her daughter, her heart. Michelle's father was one of her professors and nobody knew to this day. He'd ordered her to have an abortion and the order had been punctuated with the worst beating she'd ever endured at his hand.

That night Michelle's father, Dr. Michael Montgomery, drove her in his shiny black Cadillac to the rickety old clapboard house on the outskirts of Tupelo, Mississippi as she sat in the front seat sobbing. She knew she'd never be able to get back home from there without him and he said he'd pick her up in the morning. She was trapped. Ella Jean had heard of women who "took care of their pregnancies." She'd never planned to be one of them. But when the door of the black Cadillac flew open and she felt the impact of the foot in her side, she landed on the dirt. The car horn honked loud and long and he sped off. With his taillight in the distance it was pitch black dark.

Dogs began to bark nearby and a single light came on in the front of the house. Ella Jean's whole body hurt. She'd been beaten by this man before. He had slapped her and punched her, but never like this. She tasted dirt from the yard mixed with her own blood but couldn't move her face to get it off of the ground. She just lay there sprawled out, face down like a broken rag doll. With the one eye that wasn't swollen shut from the punches, she saw a short frail looking figure in a doorway. The door stayed open and a yellow light came from the hallway beyond the figure that appeared to be a woman. Amidst the pain, she was grateful for the light. Then, two tall figures passed the woman and rushed down the three rickety steps. They grabbed her by her arms and legs. Their movements were fast but not harsh. They had done this before.

"Be careful with her now. Bring her in the house and put her in the backroom."

The woman's voice was stern but kind. The room was lit by a small lamp on a table next to the bed the men placed Ella Jean on. Every muscle ached and she just wanted to die. The woman appeared with a basin of water and some rags. Ella Jean was too weak and broken to talk. The woman, the boys call Miss Mary, started wiping both fresh and dried blood off of her arms and face. She put a blanket over Ella Jean and the darkness returned in the form of sleep.

When she woke up in Miss Mary's backroom bed, a sudden resolve came over Ella Jean. God was in it and she had to see it through. She would keep her baby and she'd find a way to get home. Her strength seemed to return with her resolve and although she ached all over, the sun had come up. Daddy Sloane always said the sun coming up was a second chance. She had another day to get it right. She would have to figure out just how to do it and she did.

Sitting in the Naval Academy Chapel so far away from the pain of that night and that dismal time in her life, Ella Jean felt triumphant. She was never prepared for the joy and sense of purpose motherhood brought her. Her mother, Jean seemed to hate everything about being somebody's mother. She didn't even like being called mother or mama – just Jean. But it was different for Ella Jean. She loved her baby and promised herself and God the moment the nurses brought her the tiny pale infant with the mass of curly brown hair, that she would protect her from hurt harm and danger for as long as she lived. Michelle was her life.

So being in this beautiful fancy cathedral watching her third niece get married, she was filled with the sense that she had somehow accomplished that. Pam had moved all over the world with Randolph and Ella Jean respected their marriage and their sacrifices. She and her sister were different in many ways, but they both loved Daddy Sloane and each other and had worked hard to be better mothers than the one they'd had.

Chapter 13

....

Michelle was pissed off that she had to be there. She smoothed the lap wrinkles in her pale green Michael Kors skirt suit and pretended to read the program. Aunt Pam was a snooty bitch who thought everything she and those damn "R" named daughters did was news. Retched, Raggedy, Ratchet and Rat-face was what they should have been called. She thought she was going to die of embarrassment from her mother's ugly navy blue polyester dress and jacket ensemble and that she'd faint from all the damn cheap perfume Ella Jean had bathed herself in to honor this joyous occasion.

Ella Jean crossed her small feet clad with vinyl navy blue low heeled pumps and held the matching blue purse close to her bulging stomach. She wasn't sloppy fat, but she was a solid size twenty on a good day and stood only five feet two inches tall. She turned and smiled at her lovely, college educated daughter, oblivious to Michelle's shame and hateful thoughts. Her love for Michelle and pride in her accomplishments was blinding. When it came to Michelle, Ella Jean simply chose to see only what she wanted to see.

Michelle was everything she was not. Her daughter was tall and thin, with light skin and thick shoulder length hair. When Michelle was young the lady at the beauty salon had called it "good hair." That didn't sit too well with Ella Jean because she thought all hair was "good hair" if it was your hair and on your head. Even the synthetic fiber wig full of brown and red highlights and curls she was wearing now was "good hair" because it was hers. She paid for it. Ella Jean smiled at the foolishness of her thoughts and focused on Pam and her niece René and the wonderful mothers the two of them had become. They had raised beautiful daughters and the cousins would always have each other. She couldn't wait to get home and tell her boss and good friend, Reverend Franklin, about her niece's grand wedding. Pam and Randy sure did put on the hog for this one.

Rachel, Reagan and Rae stood in their mint green chiffon gowns and tried to paint on expressions that did not reveal what they were actually thinking. Ever-practical Rachel thought the wedding was lovely and wondered if her parents were okay financially. She made a mental note to check with Dad about their financial health later in the week.

Reagan thought about her own wedding to Sean just four years ago. She thought about how small it was and how glad she was that they'd had a destination wedding in Istanbul and that many of the fake people attending René and Jared's wedding were not there. She felt pleased about that. Even if Sean's mother had acted a fool and faked a heart attack because the wedding wasn't going to be held at her beloved Abyssinian Baptist Church in New York, it all worked out.

Rae was tired of standing and thought about how ugly the gowns were and what a waste of good money the whole wedding business was. Weddings and funerals were, in her opinion, the biggest rip-offs in the world. She stared at Jared, trying to read his mind and read his past. He was a hard nut to crack. But she was confident that she'd find out who he was and what he really wanted with her sister before it was too late.

The Chaplain stood before René and Jared as they looked into each other's eyes, both lost in private thoughts. Jared thought about how different his life would be with René by his side. His thoughts trailed off to her beautiful skin and the smell of her thick hair. He'd won her. She was the prize. He was marrying the daughter of one of the most promising captains in the United States Navy. He'd beat out all the other guys, even Tony Green. They all thought he didn't know. But he was nobody's fool.

He could tell by what Tony didn't say and how uncomfortable René seemed whenever Tony was around that something was up. Jared hired a private investigator last year and got the results in a matter of days. They dated in Atlanta for a brief period and kept it hush-hush. He didn't care and wasn't about to let on that he knew. That was the past. Tony had lost her and he'd won her. She was going to be his wife in a matter of minutes. Both Tony and René were too noble and too Christian to cheat. So the deed was about to be done. Jared convinced himself at that altar that he deserved happily ever after and that it was within reach.

René thought about the words the chaplain said, "To have and to hold." That's what she wanted. She trusted Jared and he needed her. He was all alone. She didn't know where his parents were. Maybe he was lying, maybe they weren't missionaries. She didn't care and she promised herself after the incident with Tony to try to trust more. She was not about to let Jared pay for Tony's mistakes.

What she did know was that he had never cheated on her. He loved her, and perhaps most important of all, he needed her. Dr. Tony Green obviously didn't need her. He had come from a good solid family and with his looks and being an M.D.; he was at the top of the food chain. He could have his pick of any number of beautiful women, but she had taken herself out of the running. Jared really needed her. He needed her and that made her feel alive and necessary. She would help him to succeed just as her mother had assisted her dad. She'd seen the role of a navy wife up close and personal. She knew she could do this. They'd be happy.

Chaplain Brown's booming voice almost created an echo in the huge sanctuary, disrupting everyone's thoughts.

"Do you Jared take René to have and to hold, to cherish and to love in sickness and in health, for richer or for poorer, promising to put her above all others until death do you part?"

Jared promised with, "I do."

Chapter 14

....

They'd done it. The ceremony went off without incident and both the Officer's Club and the tent were aglow with soft jazz drifting from the musicians on the band stand and the sound of happy people eating free food and drinking free booze. Pam took it all in from her table near the front. Everything was perfect. Shayla had delivered. The Lord blessed.

Rachel and Trent danced while Reagan stood by the bar with Sean grinning and getting more wine. Rae was not in sight but Pam knew she was somewhere near. She had a couple of midshipmen attending the wedding as her guests that she halfway dated or considered friends or something. Pam couldn't keep up with the way relationships were defined or not defined. She hoped they weren't "friends with benefits," which she'd just last week learned meant sleeping with someone without commitment. There was nothing new under the sun. In her day that was just called being "fast" or "easy" or worse.

The receiving line, introductions and first dance had all been completed. Pam knew everyone was wondering where Jared's parents and friends were. She couldn't do anything about that. It was what it was. If he said they couldn't come then, she'd have to believe him. It wasn't a crime not to have a lot of friends. Jared said he was an only child and had grown up with various relatives when his parents answered the Lord's call to become missionaries and travel to Brazil's eastern Amazon.

Despite all of this, they looked happy. René was beaming in her Vera Wang knock off wedding dress. It was decidedly southern and made her look like a cinched waisted southern bell. René didn't believe in wasting money and had insisted on not paying thousands of dollars for a dress. Pam supposed that frugality was another place she and her father met. Jared looked handsome in his white dress uniform with his blond hair and spring tan. His usual distant look and cockiness were gone. He seemed to be, for once, in the moment as he held on tightly to René's waist as they moved from table to table to greet their or rather, her guests. They kissed, cooed and smiled.

Pam sat with Randolph, his parents, his brother Rudolph, his wife Sharon and Ella Jean and pushed the filet mignon and fingerling potatoes around on the gold- rimmed plate. The musicians and Shayla signaled that it was time to cut the cake.

Randolph teased his brother and father,

"Gentlemen, now you get to eat $1,500 wedding cake!"

The men all chuckled and Pam's father-in-law teased,

"Son, I always wanted to, always wanted to."

Pam, her mother-in-law, Elizabeth (who had started the trend and insisted on all the "R" names) and Ella Jean all laughed; each woman masking her real thoughts. Pam irritated with Randolph for harping on how much things cost and for talking about it. In her mind, it was in poor taste. Elizabeth was proud that both sons were successful with beautiful families, a corporate vice president and a senior naval officer. She felt her granddaughter deserved a $1,500 cake and more. Ella Jean was thinking about the fact that as the fulltime church secretary at Greater St. Mark Tabernacle Church of God, after taxes even with her recent raise, that the cake cost the exact same as her monthly take- home pay.

Chapter 15

….

Jared was happier than he'd ever thought possible. He was on the come up. He married into the family of an A- list naval officer with all the right connections. His wife was everything a man could want and everything his mother was not. She was smart, classy, beautiful and exotic. When he was with René, he felt like James Bond. He was double O damn seven. Even her name was exotic. Most importantly, she wasn't a drunken meth whore, like his mother. She loved him and because she was so kind and generous, when he was with her he felt as if he was too. It's like she spilled over into his emptiness and filled him up with something good. She wasn't poor white trash and with her, he'd never be seen as that again.

Grinning at her as he shoved expensive cake in her mouth he felt like he'd finally won. René laughed and the photographers snapped pictures.

"Are you happy, Mrs. Reed?" Jared crooned.

She said nothing, shaking her head up and down grabbing his face with both hands; she planted the sweetest raspberry filling kisses on his mouth. Jared felt like he was almost free and the promises he'd made to himself all those years he'd struggled were about to come true. He just had to take care of a few details and get the money they needed to be set for life. Just then he saw the answer to his problems in the corner of the tent waiting by the club entrance, just as they'd planned.

Anne, sipping a glass of champagne and soaking up the sweetness of the wedding reception, saw the tall man enter the tent at the exact same time Jared did.

"René, I've got to go to the bathroom baby," he lied.

"Okay sweetie, but hurry back. You get to take my garter off next in front of all these good people."

She laughed and kissed him once more before he hurried towards the man in the charcoal gray suit waiting by the door to the club. René never noticed the man.

As she was about to get more champagne, Tony Green approached her. He'd waited and watched for Jared to leave because he wanted an opportunity to congratulate her privately. She saw him coming but knew walking away was not an option. It would appear rude. She had nothing to hide. René accepted his hug that lasted a couple of seconds too long. Pulling away from the embrace she smiled stiffly. Tony winced.

"Congratulations, René. You're a beautiful bride. Jared is a lucky man."

"Thank you, Tony. I'm glad you came. Jared has so few friends. I know it means a lot to him that you're here today."

Tony started to ask her did it mean anything to her that he was there but thought better of it.

"Yeah, Jared's a good guy. I wouldn't have missed this for the world."

The silence was uncomfortable and René just wanted him to leave. *Walk away. You made your choice. You slept with my crazy cousin Michelle because I was practicing abstinence and you were a horny butt fart, Dr. Tony Green. Walk away.* The thoughts whirled around in René's head and she willed him to read her mind. He didn't.

"Your parents look great, Tony, it's always good to see them and your little brother looks like a grown man. Is he a sophomore or junior now at Wake Forest?"

Tony thought, *so that's the way it is? We are going to do the small talk thing and play nice. You accuse me of something I didn't do, stop taking my calls and avoid me. I don't see you other than at family gatherings and you refuse to be alone with me to talk. The next thing I know, you've met and fallen in love with Jared Reed, of all people.* Tony thought Jared was okay, a squared away guy and everything, but not anybody he could see René with. He wasn't her type and he wasn't good enough. René and her entire family, including her aunt Ella Jean, were practicing Christians. Jared was a wild party dude who had no room for deities or religion in his life. Jared was a hungry hustler. Tony just wanted to know how all this happened, how things went so terribly wrong.

"Yes, Eric's twenty now. He's just finished his junior year. Well listen, I just wanted to tell you how happy I am for the both of you. Congratulations again René," with that he turned and walked away.

René watched him walk across the chiffon draped tent. She wasn't sure what to feel but she wasn't going to let two timing Tony Green spoil her wedding day. Who did he think he was? Acting all wounded. *He cheated!* Michelle had met her for lunch and showed her all the filthy texts messages he'd sent her. She'd told her when and where their nasty little trysts had taken place and spared no details. René knew more than she wanted to know about Tony Green and her crazy cousin, Michelle Washington.

Michelle had seen the encounter from her table and got up to intercept Tony before he could get to the bar. She jumped up and wrapped her arms around him planting a kiss square on his lips and squeezing his butt cheek with her spiny fingers. René witnessed this and promptly turned away to find her husband. Tony shook his head and released himself from Michelle's grip.

"How've you been, Michelle?" He was polite.

"I'm fine, Tony. You can see that, can't you?" Michelle stepped back to give him the full view.

Tony wanted to know why René thought he'd slept with her and he'd asked her back when it happened. Michelle's answer was always the same. She had no idea where René got that idea or any of her other ideas. Michelle claimed René had always been a bit insecure and jealous of her. Before he went back to Atlanta, Tony wanted to know what the hell was really going on. Okay, it was too late for him and René, but where did all this come from? René refused to talk about it. She just said he was filthy and not the man she thought he was and nobody she wanted in her life. That was that.

"Michelle, did you ever tell René that you and I were anything more than friends?"

Michelle looked into his eyes.

"Why would I do that, Tony? You're not my type. You're an Eagle Scout and a good boy. That's Auntie Pam and the 'four ratchets'' type. But me, I like me some bad boys. Besides, my mother has always wanted me to hook up with you or Frankie Bea and I make it a practice to never do what my mother wants me to do. So, for once and for all, the answer is no. My cousin is delusional and paranoid. She always thinks somebody wants her man. I didn't then and I don't now. We can never be anything but friends, Tony. The white boy is fine too, but don't nobody want him either."

She laughed at her joke about René's brand new husband, Jared, a bit too loud and linked arms with Tony.

"Let's get something to drink, friend."

Chapter 16

....

"Have you seen Jared?" René casually queried her brother-in-law, Trent.

"No René, did you lose your man already? Y'all ain't been married three hours yet," he teased.

René gave Trent a playful punch in the shoulder and headed outside toward the restrooms. As she approached the arched doorway, Jared was coming inside and a tall red haired man in a gray suit was leaving the club.

"Who was that?" René asked, smiling.

"Oh just someone from work," Jared slipped both arms around his new wife and kissed her soft brown cheek.

"Well I'm going to powder my nose, as mom would say, and I'll meet you on the dance floor for the tossing of the bouquet and the throwing the garter thingy."

Jared placed his palm over the key in his dress white uniform pants pocket that would unlock the safe deposit box with his money in it and headed back to their guests. He bumped into Michelle, René's cousin, as he entered the room. The music was lively and most of the women were on the floor doing some kind of line dance.

"Congratulations and welcome to the family," Michelle cooed.

There was something about Jared, she liked. He was handsome enough but there was something else. He had this hunger in his eyes that Michelle found very sexy. Michelle had the same hunger. She wanted more of everything, always. She thought, *game recognizes game and we are more alike than you know.*

Michelle was pretty and Jared was amused at how she stared so obviously and unapologetically at him. She gazed admiringly at every inch of him, making sure to linger longer on the spots decent women avoided. She sized him up every time they were together. They'd seen each other at a couple of family holiday events but he tried to keep his distance. It was made clear to him that René didn't like her cousin. He was not to like her either and so he didn't. He didn't care one way or the other. René was all he wanted.

"Thank you for the welcome." He pulled his hand out of her grip.

Michelle reached into her Betsey Johnson rhinestone clutch and pulled out a card. She extended her hand and placed the card into Jared's palm.

"Here, you're going to need this. The deeper you get into our lovely family the more you'll need support and lots of booze. Call me. I can help you make sense of it all. I've got all the major players figured out and an open bar."

Just then Rae appeared from what seemed like nowhere. She bounce up to the pair and smiled.

"Hey brand new brother-in-law, what's up?"

"Hello Michelle, this was a beautiful wedding wasn't it? I guess you're next, any prospects?"

Jared said nothing and hated that Rae was always snooping. She was a brat and he didn't have the patience for her psycho babble and pseudo intellectual superiority. She had been sheltered and pampered. She had the luxury of exploring theories. Reality was whipping his butt from the minute he came into this world and he simply couldn't relate to this girl or girls like her.

Michelle broke the silence,

"Hello sweetie. No, Cousin Michelle has no prospects at the moment but I am working on a few things."

She gave Jared a tricky grin, chuckled and walked away.

Rae smiled sweetly,

"Strange bird that one. You wanna get a drinky drink, Jared?"

Jared linked arms with Rae,

"Don't try to play me, grasshopper. You are under age and I'm not going to start my first official day in the family contributing to juvenile delinquency."

She grinned.

"It was worth a try."

Rae winked and skipped off like a ten year old kid. As the flowing strapless chiffon gown waved in her wake, she looked as if she was playing dress up.

René joined her new husband and lovingly led him by the hand to the center of the room. All eyes were on them and there was a drum roll. Rachel approached her sister and handed her the ribbon-clad bouquet of pink and green calla lilies. René raised it over her head with her back turned to the army of single women that had gathered to make the catch. Michelle was on the front line and pushed some really skinny girl to the floor to grab the flying flowers. Rae stood off to the side, refusing to join such antifeminist rituals and scoffed.

"Desperate heifer."

Just then her Aunt Ella waddled over to join her.

"Look a der! Ain't it good Missy caught the bouquet? I sho hope she git married soon and I hope it's Tony. Don't you think they make a good couple, Rae? Well she's getting up in age and I sure hope the two of them get married soon." Ella Jean beamed.

"Yes, Aunt Ella Jean, I think they would make a great couple." Rae lied.

She had learned years ago, who could handle truth and who ran from it. She loved her Aunt Ella Jean. She was generous, kind and sweet. But when it came to her daughter, Michelle, her "Missy," she had a blind spot. She only saw what she wanted to see even when it clearly wasn't there. They stood there in silence for a while until Pam approached her sister and youngest daughter.

"Michelle looks lovely, Ella Jean. She really does. You've done great by her. I hope she gets married soon. I know she was thinking about med school but I think the master's in public health was the perfect degree for her. She seems to be happy. Is she happy, Ella Jean?"

"Pammy, I think so. I just wish she wasn't so independent. She hardly ever wants me around. She's not like your girls who want to be with you all the time. I just want her to not be alone. I ain't gettin' no younger and I won't always be here. She doesn't even have any girlfriends. I want her married off and happy."

Rae started to go into a rant about the foolishness of thinking a woman needed a man to be happy but she thought better of it and didn't say anything. Ella Jean went to congratulate Michelle on catching the bouquet as Michelle made a dash from the room. The garter toss was over and it landed on the floor as the eligible men leaped as far from the airborne undergarment as they possibly could get.

"Dumb nasty customs." Rae spoke to her mother who seemed lost in a world of her own. Pam just smiled.

"So, who was the man that came to see Jared today but didn't come into the reception?"

Pam smiled harder, "I don't know, but I'm sure it's nothing for you to be concerned about."

Rae leaned in closer and whispered.

"I overheard him tell René, it was someone from work, but the guy in the suit put something in the palm of his hand that I couldn't make out and Jared put it in his pants pocket."

Staring seriously at her mom, she continued.

"First of all, civilians that work for the military usually don't have on suits on Saturday at two in the afternoon. Secondly, Mom, what was in his pocket? Come on? That doesn't seem fishy to you? Is he buying drugs?"

"Stop snooping. Make yourself useful and go help Shayla catalogue the wedding gifts."

Rae walked away even more determined to keep an eye on Jared Reed. Something was up and she was going to get to the bottom of it.

Part II

SUMMER

The Promise of Pain

Chapter 17

....

As sunlight crept in through the slits in the white hospital blinds, vivid horizontal light cast shadows. In pain and groggy with drugs, Michelle groaned, "What day is it?" The digital clock on the nightstand stood out among the creature comforts. There was the pink plastic pitcher for water and a cup along with an odd-shaped pan to pee in or spit in or something. Michelle squinted thinking this would be the same time she'd be getting up to let her dog Sheba out. She wondered who was taking her out for her daily walk this morning.

What happened? She remembered the car, the hot July air with the windows down. Sheba was perched on her lap barking and Michelle was laughing too. Jared's mesmerizing smile still lingered in her mind. It was the last thing she remembered. Michelle believed they were happy and the weekend promised to be special. Three years had flown by since he stood before God and man and pledged his love to her cousin René. Everything had changed and it was nobody's fault. Michelle hoped that after sleeping with Jared regularly for a year that this would be the weekend he told her he wanted out of his marriage.

René was going to be in New York working and her "high siddity" folks would be occupied with finalizing their move from the Naval Academy to their home in Virginia Beach. Their three-year tour was up and it was time to move again. She felt no sympathy for them moving all the time the way her mother did. There would be yet another military change of command for Uncle Randolph, perhaps the last one. So what? What was the big deal about everything René and that stupid, "royal" side of the family did?

Michelle had listened all her life to stories about the wonderful life her cousins lived. She didn't care. What she knew was cousin or no cousin; she was in love with Lt. Commander Jared Foster Reed and was going to be with René's husband for the entire week. The plan was to spend the weekend together at her condo in Annapolis and then drive to Charleston where Jared had a conference and they would enjoy work for him and rest for her by day, and hot steamy sex and each other's company by night. That was the plan and she was thrilled to get his call even if it was after midnight. She picked him up, just like always at the Alex Haley Memorial at the circle near Main Street. Michelle had never loved any man the way she loved Jared. The fact that he was married to her Aunt Pam's daughter, her cousin, just didn't matter. The fact that she was a few years his senior didn't matter either. Perhaps it intensified her feelings and made her love him all the more. Michelle had used many men before but this feeling was new.

Struggling to put together the pieces of last night, she squeezed her eyes together tightly and tried to conjure up details of the evening. She remembered speeding down West Street heading for Spa Road to her condo, anticipating and planning each moment in her head. They would sleep 'til noon and she'd wear her new red silk teddy that Jared sent her from Victoria's Secret along with dozens of roses for Valentine's Day to make up for having to celebrate it on the 15th of February. They had the entire weekend before his conference at the Naval Station in Charleston.

She'd planned to order Jared's favorite- fried rice from China 1 and she had stocked the bar with lots of Captain Morgan rum and there were plenty of Cokes in the fridge. Michelle could remember that when she got to the parking lot of Annapolis Elementary School on West Street right before the circle, she got out of the car and got into the passenger seat to let Jared drive her BMW. He drove with reckless abandon with his hand firmly planted on her upper thigh. She was wearing jeans, Coach sandals and a powder blue cotton camie. She could remember Sheba standing on her lap with her head hanging out the window, her white mane blowing and her tongue hanging out as if airing itself. They were listening to The Steve Miller Band, *Fly like an Eagle.* All was right with the world, and then – nothing. Somebody hit the off switch.

Now all she heard were the whispers. Nurses with bad attitudes were wading in and out of the room like zombie robots. A strong male voice, she assumed was the doctor, said the other driver was a woman too and that she was on another floor in the hospital and expecting to do fine after minor surgery. She heard him then say, "Ms. Washington is a lucky woman to have survived with broken ribs, trauma to her liver, just a few bruises and a seatbelt cut on her shoulder."

"That airbag saved her life," a soft female voice with a New York accent said, flatly.

She needed to know how long she had been asleep and where Jared was.

Chapter 18

....

"Missy, it's me Mama, I been here all morning just prayin' over you. I knew God would come through." Sharp pain shot down the left side of Michelle's body to mix with the irritation and disdain she felt from hearing her mother's voice.

Shit. Who called her? How'd she get here from Pascagoula? She wanted to say something, but no words would come.

"They say you broke four ribs and the car is busted up bad." To her, Ella Jean's words sounded like chalk on a board in slow motion.

Her mother was decidedly southern. Michelle Washington wondered how it was possible to sound poor. She got the fact that her mother's cheap polyester size 20 pantsuits, rocked over cheap faux leather shoes and matching purses branded her. She didn't open her eyes and knew the ensemble today would be purple or bright orange. Years ago, when she was at Howard, in D.C., the girls had called her mother's clothes "loud" after her first visit for parents' weekend. She never invited her again.   Her mother looked poor and she got that, but the sound of Ella Jean's voice advertised, "country broke busted." It seemed to scream that they somehow were not good enough.

"Missy, I know you can hear me. The Reverend and his son be back directa. They was nice enough to drive me to you. You know Frank Jr. got a lot of feelins for you. They was good enough to drive me to my baby. That's right. Missy, you all I got in dis world." Ella Jean patted Michelle's slender light brown perfectly manicured hands with her own rough fat sausage like fingers.

Michelle opened her eyes just enough to take in the lay of the land. She could see only deep chocolate Ella Jean standing too close to her in a bright purple pantsuit that hugged every fat roll and a matching floral blouse. Michelle felt instantly assaulted by the familiar childhood aroma of cheap Tussy deodorant and Sulfur 8 Hair Oil. Ella Jean's bra was at war with her enormous breasts and the breasts were winning smartly. Her lavender gold studded Payless purse hung over her shoulder as if it contained the crown jewels of England. She even carried her purse to the altar when she prayed at church. "Trust God, but no man," was the creed she lived by. She had been hurt by too many people in her life. Ella Jean believed there were as many thieves in the church as on the street and always governed herself accordingly.

Her ensemble was completed with cheap gold vinyl low-heeled shoes and a synthetic copper colored wig, manmade fibers from head to toe, literally. The lights were off and the familiar banter of the local television news anchors let her know they were at Anne Arundel Medical Center.

"I called Tony and he be here as soon as he can," Ella Jean reassured. *This is one of the many reasons I hate my mother,* Michelle thought. *Why does every damn body we know have to be a part of whatever happens to me?* Tony or Doctor Anthony

Green was the last person she wanted to see and the last person she wanted to see her. She'd tricked him once and was done with him. Plus he knew Jared too well and eventually he'd catch on to the two of them. She couldn't and wouldn't risk it.

Reverend Moses Franklin and his fat monster of a son Frankie Bea burst through the door and in Michelle's mind, the room instantly got smaller. She thought of Reverend Franklin as the portly personification of "back woods preacher." Reverend Franklin had a kind heart and a deep love for God but he was a man whose day had passed and whose sphere of influence was small. His little clapboard church sat on a dirt road. It was old but neat and had 100 members on the church roll and fifty parishioners worshipping on any given Sunday. They took in about $400 a week in offerings and tithes and after paying the church bills he often used his own money from his pension and social security check to pay Ella Jean's salary.

Reverend Franklin was in love with Ella Jean and had been for as long as Michelle could remember. Everybody saw it but Ella Jean. To her he was just her friend and her personal spiritual guru. She believed his mouth to be a prayer book that held infinite wisdom and sacred truth. Michelle didn't think much of him and had once said to her mother after Ella Jean shared some particularly sacred nugget of truth he'd preached on Sunday,

"For God's sake, the man named his son Frankie Bea Franklin. How wise could he be, Mom?"

The feminine, "Bea" for a middle name was said to be after the boy's mother who died trying to get his fat ass into the world. The first and last names are self-explanatory

Chapter 19

....

To Michelle, the room now smelled like pork fat and bad memories of Frankie Bea expressing his love for her every chance he got. For years growing up Michelle ran from Frankie Bea Franklin's attempts to "make her his woman." They were friends and played in the dirt when they were little poor Mississippi kids. He was still playing in the dirt and Michelle wanted no parts of it.   He was a nice guy but he was not even on her radar screen.

Michelle called him "a big fat farmer." Frankie Bea had about ten acres in rural Mississippi. He'd started working to buy the land little by little when he was in high school and kept adding acreage. He grew corn, watermelon and sweet potatoes and made a decent living. He and his dad had a standing fishing date every Tuesday. Michelle had always vowed that she would be damned to hell before she lived that Green Acres shitty life with him. She wanted more and she'd made that perfectly clear to him the last time they talked.

Her thoughts of pitiful Frankie Bea Franklin were interrupted by the booming country voice of his father.

"Mornin', mornin', praise the Lord," was the Reverend's general greeting to all the rooms' inhabitants.

"God is good," he exclaimed, glancing towards Ella Jean as he moved closer to the hospital bed.

"...all the time," Ella replied on cue.

Her daughter lay there thinking. *Let the damn games begin. Look at these ignorant religion dependent fools and their dog and pony show. If there is a God, he surely doesn't know nor does he care about the likes of them, and they definitely don't know him.*

Michelle didn't believe in God. She was her own God. If God was so good, then she wouldn't have been born to an unwed poor country fat woman. If God was so good then where was he when she was enduring the whispers and the teasing for not having a father and not knowing who or where he was? Where was he when Aunt Pam and Uncle Randolph were vacationing with their four ratchets all over Europe while she sat in hot and dusty Mississippi dreaming of being anywhere but there?

She let out an audible, "umph" as she thought, *God sure wasn't good to little nappy headed bastard Michelle!*

Michelle hated church too. To her, it was a crutch for weak minded people. She hated everything about going to church and everything corporate worship represented. She'd grown up having to go just about every time the church doors were opened. She did homework during Wednesday night bible study. She passed notes in the choir stand when she sang in the youth choir on Sundays. At youth usher training on Saturdays, she daydreamed of getting out of Mississippi. But as she grew into her teens she spent most of her time at church avoiding Frankie Bea.

"She sho look good for all she been thew," spit Reverend Franklin.

"She sho do, she sho do." Her mother's voice trailed off as she patted Michelle's hand. Ella Jean reeked of a foul combination of Tussy deodorant, Jean Naté cologne, Noxzema and Jergen's lotion. Each product alone was okay. Together, it was altogether too much for Michelle, the perfect metaphor for Ella Jean Washington.

"Well baby, we gon be gettin' back to the motel to check out and I'm a get the keys from yo pocketbook and we be der at yo place gettin' thangs ready for you to come home. Plus Tony be here soon and you gon be fine den, yes indeed."

Michelle winced, willing herself, to no avail, to jump up and run for her brown Coach tote to prevent her mother from nabbing the keys and going through her stuff. But she couldn't move so she just lay there feeling pissed and helpless. Ella Jean kissed her only daughter sweetly on the forehead and turned to lead her entourage of fat folks out of the room. Michelle wondered if Ella Jean would take care of Sheba.

"Mama," she called faintly as Ella Jean's greasy sausage puffed fingers overwhelmed the brass door knob. Ella Jean turned as did Reverend Franklin and Frankie Bea.

"Will you take care of Sheba, she's my dog, a little white Maltese, has…any…body…mentioned…my baby? Where is she?"

Ella Jean gave a puzzled glance to the diminutive nurse standing in the corner trying to be invisible. Fearing her child delusional and worse off than she'd been told, she barked softly,

"Hush up, Chile, won't no dog in the car. The police said you was alone. Save yo strenf, hear." She led the recessional into the hall and the door closed softly.

In the hall Ella mumbled to God, herself and Reverend Franklin,

"Lord, help me ta help my po' child; what's all this talk about a dog?"

Reverend Franklin assured her it would be okay with one of his favorite biblical quotes.

"He ain't gonna put on you more than you can bear."

The fact that this appears nowhere in the bible mattered little to either of them. It was the idea of it that they found comforting. They operated in a belief system untouched by conventional wisdom.

Frankie Bea silently walked behind them as they each went into their separate mental spaces. Ella Jean, consumed with worry about Michelle, Revend Franklin on what it would be like to sleep with Ella Jean and Frankie Bea Franklin hoping he'd get some time alone to talk to Michelle, and excited that he was going to be in *her* house finally, even if she wasn't there. He, unlike the other two, wondered about her dog. He knew Michelle better than anyone did. The urgency in her voice was real. There was a dog, and he aimed to find it for her.

Chapter 20

....

The room seemed cooler and darker as a result of the exit of the three stooges: her mother, Reverend Franklin and his country son, Frankie Bea. Michelle lay there trying to remember the details of the car accident. She remembered that West Street was practically deserted. Jared was laughing and telling her how much he couldn't wait to get her home. The nurse said her car was hit head- on by a Chevy Suburban. Some midshipman working Plebe Summer was driving with his mom and trying to get back on the yard before curfew. She looked down at her hand and saw cuts, scratches and purple and blue marks reaching up her arm. If she could just call Jared he'd fill in the gaps in her memory.

Why was this turning out this way? Michelle's anger began to slowly accelerate. Why was her mother here and Tony on the way? She didn't want to see Tony Green. Just because his practice was in Annapolis and he had hospital privileges at the medical center, didn't mean he needed to be called to save the day. He was not her knight in shining armor as her mother thought. She'd only used him to spite René. She tricked René nearly five years ago. It all began with a lie and it ended with a lie.

She never had any intention of going to anybody's damn medical school. Michelle tried to shift her body to get up but fell back down onto the bed with a thud, grinning at the thought of her "affair" with Tony. It had all been made up. When she visited Atlanta to tour Emory for grad school she'd called him and asked to meet and talk about medical schools, the MCATs and options in public health. Tony had taken the bait. They'd gone to lunch at Pascal's.

She was already sitting in a booth along the brick wall of the restaurant wearing a soft black cardigan without a bra and the top three buttons undone. Tony walked in with a black leather jacket, jeans and a crisp robin's egg blue oxford shirt flashing his beautiful smile. Michelle thought, *"Damn, he is good looking."* Tony leaned down and pecked her cheek taking in her exposed light brown flesh.

"Michelle, all grown up!" He bellowed. "I haven't seen you since René's debutante thing with Jack and Jill. How you been, girl?"

Michelle smiled.

"You look good too, Dr. Tony! Don't mention that crazy Jack and Jill mess Aunt Pam had my cousins roped into."

She thought about how they were always inviting her to some damn teen event. Any excuse to show off the four "ratchet" cousins and magnify the fact that she didn't belong. In an effort to include her, she got their sympathetic invitations. She'd lived with pity for a long time, but not anymore. Things were about to change. Tony interrupted her thoughts by pretending to be offended.

"Hey, you're talking to a Jack and Jill legacy here. Watch yourself, my feelings are easily hurt!"

They both laughed and broke the tension. The pair enjoyed their lunch of Pascal's famous fried chicken as Michelle listened to Tony's guidance about medical schools. She knew full well that she had no intention of attending. Michelle was triumphant in her sickbed reminiscing about the way she broke Tony and René's little love affair up. She didn't have an ounce of remorse.

It had been so easy. After that first lunch she'd invited him to her hotel the next night to have dinner and talk some more. He was hesitant but felt sorry for her and he wasn't sure why. Tony Green was a sweet and caring man. He'd give you his last. So Michelle met him in the hotel restaurant and listened once more to medical school drivel. As he talked she reached her hand into his jacket pocket and slipped his cell phone out, dropping it into her open purse on the floor between his chair and hers. She laughed and he didn't hear it drop. He didn't even notice.

After a few minutes, Michelle scooped up her purse and excused herself to go to the ladies room. Tony waited, munching on calamari rings like a grazing sheep, blindly headed to slaughter. Finally in the bathroom, she placed her purse on the sink and held the locked phone close. She quickly typed in his code. When they met for lunch at Pascal's when she asked him to call her phone, deceptively claiming she'd misplaced it. Michelle then stood close to him as they were leaving and remembered, *2…4…6...8. How lame can you get?*

Michelle began texting four messages to her own number. The last one read:

Thanks Michelle - ur on fire girl. That was the best sex I ever had. U shld b a urologist bae, cuz u know ur way around the… LOL

She took a screen shot of the texts and then erased them. Next to the two restroom doors were the staff exit doors. One door was the service entrance and the other was an exit to the parking lot. Michelle slipped out of the exit door into the cool Atlanta night. She walked with a clipped pace to the two men in red jackets and black pants. Perfect. At the valet station she found her mark. He was young and hungry and listening to head phones waiting to park the next car and get the next tip. She slid up to him and placed her hand gently on his shoulder.

"Baby, I need a secret favor, I need you to be my ninja," she whispered, smiling seductively.

"What is a secret favor?" He grinned.

"It's something you're gonna do for me and it's gonna be just between you and me. On top of that, it's going to be good for you, too."

He looked amused and about twenty years old. Michelle quickly placed Tony's cell phone into the guy's palm. Then, she slowly reached into her low cut black dress, matching lace bra, exposing the underlying flesh. She gently pulled out a $50 bill from the three or four bills she'd stashed for safe keeping. Slipping the lone bill into his pants pocket, she squeezed his thigh.

"This phone belongs to my man. I just wanted to check up on him a little bit and find out what he's been up to. So if you could quickly put this phone back on the floor on the driver's side of the green convertible BMW 32i, I would be forever in your debt."

She waited for a response. He looked around as if to check for witnesses and nodded.

"I gotchoo."

When she returned to the table, Tony was looking for his phone. He wanted for call René and check for a message from the radiologist.

"What's wrong, Dr. Green?" Michelle asked, softly.

"I can't find my phone, I wanted to call René because we're supposed to catch a movie later. I thought it was in my pocket…" Tony patted himself down, looking for the phone.

"Did you leave it in the car? Do you want me to call it? I am forever leaving mine in my car, Tony. Remember last time it was me who lost my phone, this time it's you. Go figure." Michelle was pleasant, helpful and convincing.

"Okay, excuse me I'll be right back." Tony left to take the elevator to the parking garage in search of his cell phone. As soon as he was out of sight, Michelle sat grinning at how easily he'd been duped. She liked to work with more challenging prey. With a sigh she summoned the waiter, ordered dessert and enjoyed the first few bites of her crème brûlé. When Tony returned, frustrated and confused, he clutched his long lost phone.

"Damn, here it is. It was on the floor of my car. I must have dropped it when I was getting my keys out of the ignition."

He was happy to have it back. Michelle smiled, pleased with herself. People were so dumb and would take ownership of just about anything if you went along with it.

Chapter 21

….

A jolt of pain made her acutely aware of her surroundings and planted her firmly back in the here and now. She was in the hospital and Jared was nowhere to be found. The pain was incredible. It hurt to breathe and the thought of her mother and that *country band of fools* being at her house only made it worse.

She needed to see Jared, to talk to him. Worst yet, she couldn't ask about him because exposing the relationship now would be devastating. René was pregnant. René's father, Uncle Randolph, had some huge military ceremony coming up and Jared was up for reassignment. Michelle was certain that after the baby was born and before his reassignment Jared would leave René. She would be the one to move with him to his next duty station. She was *almost* certain of it.

"Hey Michelle, how are you sweetie?"

Tony Green poked his handsome face inside the door and stepped in smiling as usual. He was always so damn happy and that was probably one of the things that made Ella Jean so fond of him and repelled Michelle. Life wasn't all that damn happy to be smiling all the damn time. Tony began his explanation of her condition as he approached the bed.

He started talking and Michelle's head started to spin and ache. He was talking too fast and speaking in the authoritative voice reserved for his patients. Michelle didn't like this side of Tony Green, going on and on about what the admitting physician had said about the accident. He said that she'd been driving and hit a van head-on. Both the van and her BMW had been totaled and the other driver was in critical condition. Tony went on and on about some laceration of Michelle's liver caused by blunt force trauma sustained in the collision.

Standing over Michelle with her chart in his hand, he admitted to himself that she was beautiful but there was something about her he didn't trust. He smiled, looking from the chart to the bruised woman on the bed. He kind of felt sorry for her. To Tony, it seemed as if Michelle was always fighting an imaginary foe. She was surrounded by people who loved her but starving for love.

"Michelle, your chart shows a positive response to an initial fluid bolus and maintenance of a stable hemodynamic state. This was the result of the CT scan of your abdomen and pelvis. Unfortunately, Dr. Rankin identified extravasations and is considering angiogram and angioembolization if they don't stabilize. Failures of these steps may mandate operative intervention."

Michelle smacked her lips ignoring the pain in every facial movement. She was just pissed off. *Where was Jared?* There was a clear liquid dripping into her veins from the bag hanging above her. It was there to keep her from feeling pain, but she still hurt so much. She wanted to scream. She got one chance to get away with Jared for an entire week and instead of being in Jared's arms, she was in this jacked up hospital looking at Tony the clown. She closed her eyes tightly and tried to process the medical mumbo jumbo that had just escaped from his mouth.

"What the fuck, Tony?" Michelle spoke in a raspy low voice.

"Speak English. I don't know what the hell you're talking about."

Tony flinched at the harshness of her words.

"I'm sorry, Michelle. You are in the field and with your master's in public health, I assumed…"

"Don't assume, Tony. Just don't," Michelle barked, hurling at him, all the anger and hurt she felt about Ella Jean, Jared and everything else.

"Okay. Well, they will monitor you for the next few hours, possibly twenty-four. After which, surgery to sew up your lacerated liver may be necessary. The bleeding seems to have lessened and that's a good sign. That's all I know. I wish I could help more. When your mom called me she was frantic." Tony tried to offer reassurance.

Michelle closed her eyes and concentrated on breathing. This was all too much.

"Tony, does René know I'm in the hospital? Are she and Jared still in town? I heard she was working in New York this week and Jared was going to a conference. Mama said Aunt Pam was worried about her traveling alone in this last trimester of her pregnancy." There. She got it out. *Where is Jared? Get him to me!*

"I don't know, Michelle, but I can call René from the nurse's station and let her know you want to see her. I'm sure your whole family knows and is praying for you. Pam and the crew will start rolling in soon enough," he smiled.

"Is there anyone else you need me to call? Someone you're seeing – a love interest?" He tried to deliver compassion with his eyes. But it had always puzzled him that he'd never seen her at any of the social events with a date. She was always alone.

"No. There is no love interest." Michelle opened her eyes and stared at the empty wall beyond Tony.

Thou shall not commit adultery

Chapter 22

....

Ella Jean looked around Michelle's steel gray kitchen. It was just as she thought it would be, should be. It looked like a rich woman's kitchen and even though Michelle was far from rich, she lived rich and that suited Ella Jean fine. The kitchen was spotless and cold with gray walls and high-end stainless steel appliances. She pulled the refrigerator door open and realized she was looking into the freezer. It was completely empty except for two huge bottles of liquor: one, she was familiar with. It had a black label that read, *Jack Daniels* and the other a curly-haired pirate on it that said *Captain Morgan.* One was amber and one was clear like water. Ella Jean wonder, *who keeps liquor in the freezer?*

Quickly closing one door and opening the other, Ella Jean felt off-kilter by Michelle's life. Why is the freezer beside the refrigerator instead of on top of it and separated from it? This generation of women had to have everything at their fingertips and in an effort to make their lives easier, always made things more complicated. She peered inside the refrigerator staring at its lonely contents. There were two bottles of red wine, two bottles of champagne, a six pack of Coca Cola and two cans of Diet Coke. The only thing that wasn't liquid was a small container of Greek yogurt with peaches in it. Ella Jean thought, *how pitiful.* She worried about her daughter's daily life. *Was Michelle a drunk?*

She looked in the far corner of the kitchen near the sliding glass door and saw two small bowls filled with water and pet food. She walked toward the bowls and the sliding glass window to get a closer look. The bowls were stainless steel and personalized with fancy black letters that read "Sheba." So maybe Michelle wasn't delirious when she was asking about her dog. Ella Jean decided to wait and figure this out after she got settled in and ate. Michelle would come home soon and she intended to stay put until she got her daughter on her feet again. Reverend Franklin had made it clear that he couldn't be away from the church that long and would be getting on the road in the morning.

She found peace in the fact that Michelle had accomplished most of the things that Ella Jean had dreamed for herself before her own unplanned pregnancy so many years ago. She thought about the many promises she had made to herself. Ella promised herself she'd finish school and not let this one man ruin her life. She'd be an example for her smart little sister Pam and make something of herself. She hadn't gone back to school but she had poured every ounce of her energy into building a good solid life for her child.

Her attention turned to beyond the sliding glass doors of the first condo. The deck and backyard were beautiful. Michelle had huge oak trees on her neatly manicured lawn. Ella Jean looked down at the redwood stained deck and saw it. There was a tiny dead sparrow directly beyond the sliding glass door. Pushing the door open, she scooped the bird up with her hands and walked to the edge of the yard. The tiny sparrow lay stiff and lifeless in her palm, its feathers soft and still. Ella Jean stooped and gently placed the bird on the ground covering it with loose mulch. She felt guilty for the shallow grave. Everybody and everything deserved a decent burial.

Walking back towards the house she thought about the first time she started finding dead birds. The old folks said it meant somebody was going to die; it was an omen. The only person who knew about the birds was Pam. Ella Jean laughed out loud as she entered her daughter's kitchen and locked the door thinking about waiting for someone to die when she started seeing dead birds. It was her second year in college. Nobody died.

Ella Jean was nineteen-year-old home economics major. She was a sophomore away at college in Tupelo, Mississippi, when she got pregnant first semester and was big bellied by Christmas. She hadn't been in school for a month. She was so ashamed but so involved with Michelle's fast talking daddy that it just didn't matter. She thought about suicide all the time. He was mean and the meanness had come all at once as a total surprise.

Michelle was so much like him. Dr. Michael James Montgomery III was a visiting English Literature professor and she thought he would marry her and take care of she and Michelle. It started off wrong and it ended wrong. Daddy Sloane had been the only one to not ask questions, but he couldn't hide the hurt and disappointment in his eyes as he watched her belly grow bigger every day. Dr. Montgomery promised her the moon and gave her absolutely nothing.

Ella Jean sat at the glass-topped kitchen table as her stomach began to burn with hunger. Reverend Franklin would be back with the food soon. She'd sent he and Frankie Bea with a list to "make groceries" for the weekend. She'd figure out the rest later.

Grocery List

2 rotisserie chickens
2 box of 8 pc fried chicken
1 lb of deli potato salad
Glory collard greens (4 cans)
1 bell pepper
1 celery stalk
1 yellow onion
2 dozen eggs
2 lbs of bacon
1 loaf of sliced white Wonder Bread
Lipton tea bags
6 lemons
Maxwell House Instant Coffee
1 lb of sugar
Carnation Milk

Chapter 23

….

Ella Jean's mind slipped slowly back to the first day in Dr. Michael Montgomery's class at Thompson College. She was a second year student and taking the required English 200 class. All her little college friends on campus talked about how handsome this professor from up north was, but she was not prepared for the elegant thirty something chocolate man that stood at the chalk board in the front of the room.

Dr. Montgomery said,

"Good morning students. My aim is to make you see the books, the English language, the world and yourselves differently from this moment forth."

He ain't never lied.

At first it was all pretty innocent. Ella Jean asked for extra help after getting a 'D' on the first test. Her subject-verb agreement and grammar in general were terrible. She wrote like she talked and she talked like everyone she knew talked- incorrectly. Daddy Sloane spoke pretty good English but he was the only one. Her teachers had talked "proper" and Ella Jean never considered mimicking the way they spoke. It had never even occurred to her, because she saw them as so different from herself. But now, away from all of them, she felt she could be anyone she wanted to be, and was excited about being a home economics teacher. Ella Jean was excited about the idea of making Daddy Sloane and Pam proud.

So the third week of September she walked up to his desk in her starched white blouse, black skirt hugging her shapely hips, wearing white bobby socks and penny loafers. She was all of one hundred and twenty pounds at 5'3". Her neat black hair was pulled up into a French roll, carefully crafted and secured with countless hair pins. The front oversized bangs swept across her forehead grazing her left eye. She was timid and uncomfortable. He was everything she was not and everything she thought college would help her become.

He was smart. She was dumb. He was rich, compared to her and she knew she was dirt poor. He was a third generation college graduate. Everybody knew about his daddy and his granddaddy and their work establishing the chemistry department at Thompson College in Tupelo, Mississippi. His mother's father and grandfather had been medical doctors. He was the only son of two successful black people with a trail of successful black people in their wake. In contrast, her mother was a domestic worker turned stay at home drunk. She cleaned a different white woman's house each day, five days a week when she was sober enough to work and her stepdad, Daddy Sloane, worked at the paper mill like his father before him.

What impressed Ella Jean most was the way he talked. Dr. Montgomery's voice and diction sounded like a symphony, it was as smooth and as sweet as honey dripping onto your tongue. He'd gone to Thompson for his undergraduate degree and Howard University for his master's and doctorate. She was determined to get a tutor and pass his class. When she approached the corner of the desk she began to sweat. She hoped she didn't look as uncomfortable and stupid as she felt.

Ella Jean was pretty, with soft brown features and expressive eyes. Her hips were petit and round and she had full breasts and a tiny waist that brought stares and whistles. But she didn't feel pretty. She never felt pretty. Her mother, Jean, had called her so many names and beat all the confidence from her little body long before Daddy Sloane came along. She liked not being noticed, so standing at this man's desk was like climbing Mount Everest for her.

Clearing her throat she said,

"Dr. Montgomery, I really need hep with my writin' if I'm gonna evah be a school teacher."

The handsome professor looked up from the stack of papers he was grading and slowly removed his silver wire frame glasses from his face. Placing one rubber tipped end of the frame in his mouth he turned his head sideways and stared at Ella Jean. He looked her up and down slowly, taking in her soft innocence. His eyes lingered intently on her full breasts. She was uncomfortable and couldn't read what he might be thinking. He probably found her fat and disgusting and wondered why she thought she could ever be anybody's school teacher.

She felt sweaty and uncomfortable and hoped he'd assign her a tutor quickly and write down where she needed to be and when, and then call it done.

"So you aspire to become an educator, Miss Washington?"

Dr. Montgomery's question caught Ella Jean off guard. This was not supposed to be a conversation. This was supposed to be the assigning of a tutor and Ella Jean taking a seat. She moved her head, nodding up and down in quick motions like a bobble head in a rear-view mirror.

"Well, the schedules of all my graduate assistants are full and we have no tutors available at this time."

He put his glasses back on which Ella Jean took as a signal that the painful exchange was over. She turned swiftly and started back to her seat towards the rear of the classroom. She was interrupted by his arrogant articulation:

"But Miss Washington, perhaps we could work something out."

She turned towards him and stood frozen without uttering a word. Her hope was that he would be able to read her face, see that she wanted to know what the heck he was talking about and just say it.

"See me after class, Miss Washington, and we shall discuss the matter further."

He dismissed her for the second time, but this time it was for real as he focused all of his attention on the stack of papers in front of him and began marking them with his red pen. Ella Jean walked briskly back to her seat and slid into her chair. Her head was starting to pound and she had no idea what to expect. She hoped he could find a way to help her make something out of herself. Passing this class would be the beginning of that for her. It was step one.

Chapter 24

....

The classroom was quiet and Ella Jean stared at the
clock perched on the wall exactly four feet above *"Dr.
Wonderful's"* head. All heads were down, everyone was busy
writing as he graded papers. The clock struck 5 which it
signaled the end of the class period. This was Ella Jean's last
class for the day. Students gathered their papers and books
and began filing out of the room. Ella Jean stayed put until
the last student, a tall gangly boy, closed the door. Then she
looked up to see if she should go to her professor or just wait
for him to come to her. He motioned with his hand for her to
approach the desk.

She moved swiftly to the massive mahogany altar. He
didn't move but began to speak.

"Miss Washington, I am in need of assistance in a
certain area and you are in need of tutorial services if you are
ever to pass my class. You can't write and I am not certain on
what basis you were accepted to Thompson."

Ella Jean felt tears pool in her eyes. She wasn't
prepared for his cruel words and was confused that such
ugliness could come from such a beautiful place. She opened
her mouth but nothing came out. She wanted to say, *"I'm good
at math and science and I can learn. Anybody can."* But she said
nothing.

Ella Jean didn't believe that the way you started was the way you ended. She knew a whole lot of people back home in Pascagoula who had started off as poor as church mice and now lived in brick houses with more than one bathroom. They ate whatever they wanted, took vacations and drove Cadillac cars. No sir. She believed she could learn. She had gotten good grades in school and passed all her exams. She took the test to get in and got in. Now he was making her question the whole thing. He was smart. He knew more about making it. It seemed like he didn't believe *she* could do it.

She stood motionless and looked down at the pennies in her loafers. She could not look at him. He stood up and came around the desk. He sat on the end of the desk with one foot on the floor and unbuttoned his brown suit jacket exposing a fresh white shirt and a brown and black striped silk tie that dangled proudly. He was close enough for her to smell his cologne. She backed up a little, while he in turn leaned forward, and spoke softly.

"Miss Washington, I find myself in need of domestic services and I see that you are in dire need of tutorial services. I would like to propose a bartering arrangement – if you will?"

Ella Jean didn't know what *"bartering arrangement"* meant but she hoped he would speak plain and clear eventually so she would understand. She was determined not to confirm his assertions that she was dumb by asking him any questions. She would just have to figure it out later. So she continued to look down at her shoes. Dr. Montgomery reached out and lifted her chin with his first two fingers. His hands were cold.

"Look at me, Miss Washington. Eye contact is important. It is the sign of one who can be trusted."

Ella Jean felt one tear drop and hated herself for crying.

 "Yes sir," was all that came out and she knew it made no sense but could hardly take back the words. He must clearly think her to be some kind of simpleton.

Ignoring her tears, he pulled his hand away from her face and began scribbling on a small pad he'd taken out of his pocket. Ella Jean looked around the classroom with its pale green walls, hardwood floors and black chalkboard that stretched across the front of the room. She didn't know what was going to happen next but she had a horrible headache and had to pee. He tore the paper off the pad and pushed it towards her. She took it in her hand and read the address, date and time. Professor Montgomery spoke with authority.

 "I need someone to cook and do light housekeeping a couple of days a week and in exchange for that, I will go over your classwork with you and ensure your success in this course. Is that agreeable, Miss Washington? Are you free Tuesdays and Thursdays?"

Ella Jean nodded and guessed she was answering yes to both questions. It was agreeable and she was free.

"Okay. It's done. We will begin this Thursday. I thought you looked like a girl who could handle a little housekeeping."

He turned and began to erase the blackboard. Ella Jean stood there for a moment. She wasn't sure what to say. She didn't know what to make of this or what to do. She thought of writing Daddy Sloane, but didn't want to worry him or cause any trouble. He had his hands full with her crazy mother and trying to raise her sister Pam. She would figure it out.

Gathering her notebook, two pens, one pencil, English textbook and her black purse, Ella Jean thought about the deal she was entering. Daddy Sloane put her on the Greyhound bus to school just a few weeks ago with her clothes in one cardboard suitcase, two dictionaries, a bible, five cans of sardines and two rolls of saltine crackers. She had $40 tied in a handkerchief in her new white bra. This was the beginning of her second year. The whole purpose of going to college was so she wouldn't have to clean white folks' houses and cook for them. The tales of the kinds of things that happened to some of those poor girls behind the closed doors of their employer's houses was well known back home. Now, she had somehow agreed to cook and clean for this black man for some help with her school- work.

She walked into the hall and Dr. Montgomery never turned away from the board. It was as if he didn't see her anymore. On the way to her dorm, leaving the Language Arts building, she almost tripped over it. The bird's head was crushed and stuck to the pavement. Its wings lay pinned to its side stiff and grounded, its flying days clearly over. It was a fledging black bird. That day she saw her first dead bird.

Startled by the doorbell ringing, Ella Jean looked up from the table where she sat in her daughter's sterile kitchen. She had been crying and didn't even realize it. She wiped her eyes with the sleeve of her purple suit jacket and got up to get the door. All of the pain from that devil Dr. Montgomery all those many years ago slowed her movements and weighed her down. She thought she had buried it all, working hard all these years to keep the ugly secret from her sister, Daddy Sloane and most of all from Michelle. It had been a nightmare and she'd spent every day since she last saw him trying to forget it and make sure no man ever did to her daughter what Dr. Montgomery had done to her.

Chapter 25

....

Reaching for the polished pewter knobs to turn off the hot water, Jared stepped out of the marbled shower stall in the spacious townhouse he shared with his wife, René. Grabbing a thick red towel, he wiped his strong toned and tanned body. He opened the bathroom door to let the air in the room clear, and began combing his close- cropped blond hair without the assistance of seeing his reflection in the steam-covered mirror. Jared was handsome. At 6' 3", he was imposing and looked like a fleshed out version of the plastic Ken doll. He was fit and looked far more confident and commanding than he ever felt. The barking noise startled him.

"Come here, girl. Come on, Sheba." Jared bent to remove the overpriced rhinestone collar and placed it neatly in the back of his bathroom drawer.

He schemed, *Sheba will make the perfect present for René.* He hadn't seen her in four days. She was in New York working, but finished up earlier than she'd anticipated and would be home tomorrow. She said she was charging hard, meeting with clients and discussing portfolios. But Jared feared she was planning an exit strategy. He knew his pregnant wife wasn't happy.

"Fuck Michelle," he whispered without thinking.

In the accident he was the only passenger unharmed and lucid. A better man wouldn't have pushed his unconscious mistress into the driver's seat and bailed out of the car at the scene of an accident. But Jared knew he was not that better man. He had only loved two people in his whole life, his little brother, Joe, and René. He'd let both of them down. But in each case, he didn't mean to. So he hid in the shadows until the crowd gathered and the cops and ambulances arrived on the scene. Holding the scared little dog in his arms, he blended into the crowd until it dispersed and took a cab back to his car parked at the empty school parking lot. He wasn't sorry.

Jared thought his tryst with his wife's cousin. *With this extracurricular thing with Michelle, shit got crazy, and it was just too bad.* It was never supposed to go that far or for that long. It reminded him of one of the foolish sermons René listened so intently to on Sunday mornings. *"Sin always cost more than you expected to pay and stays longer than you expected it to stay."* Jared marveled at how his wife lived for that kind of bullshit. She wrote it down and repeated it on the way to the perfunctory Sunday "Bougie Brunch" with her family.

He never agreed with any of it. She never knew. Jared went along to get along and hid his core thoughts and feelings from René for fear that she'd be afraid of who he was, or who he was not. Jared was his own god and felt if there was a God, he sure as hell didn't give a damn about him. He sat quietly on the Sundays he had to attend the one-hour worship service at the Naval Academy Chapel and pretended to listen.

He'd been doing that for as long as they'd been married. It was prudent to attend church. It was good for his image, nothing more and nothing less. Lately he made mental to-do-lists, and thought about having sex with Michelle while the chaplain warned of the dangers of sin and the promise of salvation. It was easy to drown out the choirs "Blessed Assurance" with his own thoughts. Although Jared loved René he knew now that in marrying her he had gotten more than he was prepared to have.

Jared loved educated black women and everything about them. He loved their rhythm and style. There was a certain wisdom and a cool, intrinsic sensuality that he couldn't quite put his finger on but knew when he was in the midst of it. René had all of that and more. As the third and most indulged daughter of Captain Randolph Michael Hamilton, she was a prize. Their accidental meeting was something he'd planned for months.

His boy, Pat, was the Executive Officer (X/O) to Hamilton when he had command of the Aegis Cruiser Yorktown-CG48. They talked from time to time about hitching his wagon to a military star, someone who was going up, and Hamilton was that guy. Pat also said that there were some other perks to being on his staff, which included being around his "bad-ass Cosby family daughters."

"These girls have it all, man. They're fine as hell but they act like white girls with black girls' asses." Oblivious to the fact that what they said was an inaccuracy and an insult to women of all races, the two men high-fived and tilted their heads back in laughter. Jared did his research and then he saw her at the Navy ball in Norfolk when he was a lieutenant junior grade (LTJG). She was waiting for some string bean geek black dude to bring her punch, some midshipman her dad was sponsoring. He was just the kind of guy a dad wants his daughter to date. He was pitiful and harmless and somewhat asexual.

Her hair was raven and sleek, pulled back in a chignon at the nape of her neck. She looked like chocolate milk, the kind you got in school as a kid, and he just stood there unable to look away. Pat was right. She had this small upturned nose and the prettiest lips, the upper one darker than the bottom and the clearest dark brown almond shaped eyes. She wore a soft pink silk gown that draped her youthful curves. The dress was slit up to the middle of her right chocolate milk thigh, a modest plunging neckline revealing the most delicious looking breasts. They were huge for her tiny back and waist but not fake. You could tell by their softness that they were not store bought. He wanted to touch them.

Jared knew she'd feel him staring soon and that he should approach and say something, but he couldn't. He just stood there and inhaled her from head to toe. There was something helpless yet capable about this girl. She looked so innocent and yet wise beyond her years. She had been sheltered and protected by her father and the insulated nature of her military lifestyle. Jared made a solemn promise to himself; he would have her and make it his mission to protect her from hurt, harm and danger for the rest of his life.

That was five years ago. Jared's feelings for René had not changed. He had simply failed and subsequently aborted the mission when he discovered that what she needed protection from most was him. He'd never meant to cheat or hit her. He just felt so damn small and left out when he saw himself reflected in her eyes.

He thought in this post-racial age of black achievement, color no longer mattered. He knew little of the culture and sequestered world of middle class blacks. René was only twenty that night when he first introduced himself to her father betting on the good Captain's manners, counting on an introduction to his lovely daughter. She was distant and polite. He thought she'd be impressed with his rank, his looks and that she'd be honored by the attention. He'd been wrong about her and so many other things.

Chapter 26

....

René, Reagan, Rachel, Rae and Pam were unlike any women he'd met before. They didn't impress easily and the four of them were tied together by some invisible, impermeable bond that he'd come to resent. Captain Hamilton was not a part of it, but he was connected to it by their mutual love for him. He was the center of it in some way. At first he smirked at their daily early morning devotions and their prayer partner phone line bullshit. But after a while, he became both jealous of it and threatened by it.

He knew René loved him and was committed to their marriage. But he knew she didn't *need* him. He'd promised himself after leaving home that he'd never need or love anyone again. Ever. Perhaps, what irritated him most was that he needed her so badly. Jared needed her to be pleased with him. He hadn't planned to, but he'd gone out on a limb and simply fallen in love with her.

With she and her family, he always felt like the outsider. He was not one of them and it had little to do with race. This was bigger than race. There was a barrier he couldn't permeate and Rachel's husband Trent, only made things worst. He was too similar to Captain Hamilton and only served to make Jared feel more like shit. He didn't talk about religion in the same way the women did but he was always in church and on some committee and helping someone in the community. All this "lift as we climb" crap pissed him off. *Where were the folks trying to lift him when he was hungry in the dark in Ruth Anne's pissy trailer all those years ago?* Jared felt like the world was climbing over him instead of lifting him.

His brother-in-law, Trent believed in service and was one of them. He was also a graduate of Harvard Law and had made partner at one of Washington, D.C.'s most prestigious law firms. He and René's oldest sister, Rachel, vacationed with other Morehouse alumni like, Spike Lee and his wife, Tonya in Martha's Vineyard. Old boy Trent's family had a house on Oak Bluffs from way back. They played on another level.

Then there was his other brother-in-law Sean, Reagan's husband. He was an accountant whose firm had been featured on the cover of Black Enterprise magazine as one of the ten most innovative new businesses. Reagan was a jazz singer and professor; they rendezvoused all over the globe. No one ever said anything but he knew what the deal was. It was more what they didn't say that mattered.

He was separated from them by something other than race. It was something bigger that he hadn't been prepared for. There was an invisible hierarchy and he was at the bottom of it. Both Trent and Sean were from well-heeled black families. They grew up with their very own little launching pads that were designed to protect them from racism and failure. They created a small elite world with black people like themselves all over the country with organizations as its foundation. This world insured them a social circle filled with "their kind of people," or as Pam so often said when speaking of whom she enjoyed socializing with, *those with similar values."*   It was predicted, predetermined, and expected that they would do well.

Jared often wondered about it. *How in the hell had the world gone so wrong that he was jealous of any black man? This age of Obama was a bitch. Who saw it coming? The black middle and upper classes had been invisible to most of the people in his world. Now he was drowning in their church anniversaries, scholarship balls, Links, Boule', sorority and fraternity bullshit, and was tired of pretending to fit it and tired of feeling inferior to them. He was tired of being the minority. It didn't feel good. There were white people in their world and plenty black people who looked white. But there were never people who'd grown up like him and done and seen what he had.*

Sheba's barking brought him back to the present and his wet, naked body.

*"You shall not **covet** your neighbor's wife. You shall not set your desire on your neighbor's house or land… or anything that belongs to your neighbor."*

Chapter 27

....

As he dried himself completely and tossed the damp towel on the sleek marble bathroom floor, Jared ambled towards the bed where his dress blue uniform was laid out like a flattened corpse on the soft comforter. Sheba sat in the middle of the king size bed, watching his every move. He sat down and began to pull his dark blue pants on and his mind drifted to a time when there were no marble floors, housekeepers or expensive cars.

Life had begun in a lone trailer, illegally sitting next to a trash dump. Ruth Anne did "favors" for the two brothers who owned the dump and thus they were allowed to stay there rent free and call the place "home sweet home." In the summer, the smell was almost unbearable. There were junk cars, old refrigerators and wash machines strewn in their yard. People dumped their trash there late at night and assumed the trailer was abandoned or a part of the office. They had cardboard taped to the windows to cover broken panes and torn sheets for curtains. They rarely had electricity because Ruth Anne never paid the bill even when she had the money, so it was easy to pass as abandoned. The tan and green trailer sat there on eight cinderblocks and looked as lonely and desperate as the people who lived there.

Jared had gone to bed hungry too many nights. He'd been in four different foster homes after Ruth Anne got busted the first time with crystal meth. He had been only two years old when they took him away the first time. The good social worker returned him to Ruth Anne six years later when Joe was born. Ruth Anne married Joe's father and convinced the state of Florida that she was a drug free reformed woman fit to raise her two boys. The marriage lasted for one year and Joe's dad was gone before the boy turned two. Ruth Anne went back to the only cure she knew to get over yet another betrayal. She reacquainted herself with her good friend, crystal meth. There would be many more boyfriends and uncles, slaps and slights since then. After each one she'd try to transform herself from helpless junkie Ruth Anne to perfect mother Ruth Anne, promising to change. She never quite made the transformation and he and his younger brother, Joseph, suffered the abuse along with her and just did the best they could. Amid rats, roaches and a revolving door of the worst kind of men, he and Joe survived. They took the beatings and hid in the rubbish outside from the drunken rage of Ruth Anne's "boyfriends" and johns.

Once, she'd taken up with a guy name Buster who was fresh out of jail. Buster stood 6' 5" and weighed about 300 pounds. He wore a navy blue mechanics jumpsuit but had never worked as a mechanic. Buster, with his dirty yellow long nails and greasy mud brown hair, seemed to hate everything and everybody. To Joseph and Jared, he was a giant. He was always mad. Always. Buster didn't work. He just laid around all day on the shit brown couch that their cat Moe had clawed the stuffing out of. He alternated with great equality getting high, whippin' Ruth Anne's ass or screwing her, in no particular order. As soon as they got home from school, it was their turn. That's when he would beat the crap out of them until he got tired or Ruth Anne distracted him with booze, a rock of crystal or herself.

Jared hated him and knew even at fourteen that one of them was going to die. He'd given up trying to protect Ruth Anne. It never worked. Invariably, she'd turn on Jared and side with whomever he was trying to stop from beating the crap out of her. But this particular day, Buster was sitting, staring at the television with an ashtray filled with cigarette butts on his lap. Moe was on the couch next to him, her green eyes closed and her mangy marmalade body curled up in a fat circle. He was smoking and watching wrestling when Jared pushed open the dirty door to their trailer. It was never locked because it had no lock. It had been broken by the boyfriend before Buster and Ruth Anne was never lucid enough to get it repaired.

He'd pushed the door too hard, and it banged against the wall, startling Moe. Moe jumped off the couch and bumped against Buster's leg, causing the ashtray to tip and ashes and cigarette butts to fly all over Buster and the couch. Jared was frozen in the doorway by what happened next. Six-year-old Joe stood on the stoop behind him. Buster grabbed Moe with his fat filthy fingers and threw her with the full force of his rage against the door frame. The cat squealed in agony less than eight inches above and to the right of Jared's head. The impact shook the trailer and she slid down as quickly as she'd flown. Moe lay still in a crumpled heap on the floor next to his foot. Blood oozed from her eyes and mouth, both wide open.

"Fuckin' cat," Buster mumbled without ever taking his eyes off the sweaty, swollen men throwing each other around in the ring.

Jared felt a hot pain begin in his legs and rise slowly to his chest. By the time the pain got to his head, he was crying. This wasn't the first time his anger had burned like a wildfire. He walked slowly into the kitchen with measured steps, burying silent sobs. Joseph came running in screaming that Moe was dead. He wailed and slobbered and ran outside towards the dump next to their trailer.

Fourteen-year-old Jared moved passed a plate of day-old Vienna sausages with flies swarming around it and passed the dishes with remnants of crappy meals dried and clinging to them in the filthy sink. With steel determination, he opened the kitchen drawer where Ruth Anne kept the knives. There were two knives and a few broken forks and plastic spoons in the drawer. He picked up the large butcher's knife with the broken fake wood handle.

Buster didn't hear and didn't care. He kept staring at the wrestling match. Jared stood a few feet from the couch and hesitated. Buster glanced at him but it was too late. Buster's ability to react was slowed by his drunken haze. Jared, fueled by his hatred of this man and all those before him, charged with his eyes wild and tearful. He plunged the knife into Buster's neck so deeply the tip broke skin on the other side.

Jared screamed, "You shit head cat killer!"

The giant of a man slumped over shattering the ashtray as it fell from the couch to the floor. His eyes rolled back in his head and blood oozed down his dingy grey t-shirt flowing onto his chest and his back like two roads leading to different paths. He was dead.

Chapter 28

….

Joe was still sobbing sitting on a rusted out tire rim at the edge of the dump. Jared called to him to get the dolly out of Buster's flat-bed and come inside. Joe obeyed Jared blindly, like always. It was just the way it was. Jared was the only person on earth he fully trusted. When the small boy reached the door, he propped the dolly by the makeshift cinderblock steps. Joe stood frozen in the door- frame staring at Buster's body bleeding on the raggedy plaid couch.

"Is he d-d-dead?" Without looking up, Jared answered.

"Help me roll him to the wheel barrel."

Jared placed his arms under Busters arms and started to pull. He thought about the heaviness of the dead body. *Dead weight.* They play on words made him smirk. Buster was too heavy, but Jared was strengthened by anger. He motioned for Joe to get on the other end of Buster. Joe began to push hard on Buster's huge butt and he hit the floor with a slump, blood trailing as they dragged him the few feet to the door. His filthy stained shirt rose up over his floppy hairy belly as it scraped along the floor. His eyes were opened and he still looked mad. The two boys struggled with the dead weight and finally got him, butt first, in the wheel barrel by laying it on its side and kicking, pushing and dragging Buster into it. He looked like he was angry about taking this ride to the dump and that made Jared laugh.

Joe stood in silence, waiting for his next directive. Jared whispered,

"Grab the other end and let's go."

They ran fast steering the wheel barrel and kicking up the dirt covered yard. Buster's head bobbed from one side to the other as if he was giving some sick salutation to the abandoned trucks, old tires and piles of rusted crap in the yard. The two boys got close enough to the dump and pushed. Buster went flying and landed in the corner of a heap of trash.

Jared sent the wheel barrel flying on top of him and began gathering tires, tossing them on top the dead man. They added pieces of scrap metal until Buster was completely covered. He was gone, buried beneath and surrounded by mounds of garbage. Jared felt a calm sense of power. He felt Buster was trash and was finally right where he belonged. He walked slowly, exhausted by the killing, to Buster's truck and got a pack of matches off the front seat. He went back to the edge of the dump as slowly as he'd left. He lit the match and walked away. The stench of burning trash and Buster filled the air.

The two boys worked in concert that day. In that instant, Jared was baptized with fire and learned something critical about himself. It was the day he knew he would move hell and high water to survive. He just wanted to survive. He didn't need a mother or father. He didn't need a god. He didn't even need his little brother. He needed to survive.

Jared walked with deliberate calm back into the trailer and began to clean up the blood on the floor with some old rags he found balled up under the kitchen sink. He walked the bloody rags to the dump next to their trailer and threw them in. *Now what to do with Buster's piece of a truck?* Jared knew the keys would be next to the bed in Ruth Anne's bedroom. He walked trance-like across the stained carpet, decorated with piles of filthy clothes. His dirty blond hair dripping with sweat, he glanced at the unmade bed and crumpled thin sheets.

He knew she wouldn't be home until late. She was at the bar and knew how to get free drinks. She'd stay as long as they were pouring. Some strange man would drop her off and she'd stumble in and start fighting with Buster. Jared knew Buster hadn't been jealous of the guys she'd been with at the bar during those fight nights. The tension was really because they were both drowning in their own misery and desperation, like two trapped animals. Well, he had just set one of them free.

Chapter 29

....

Jared had to get to Joe to tell him to keep quiet about Buster and Moe. Jared knew that if Joe started talking about their cat, he would eventually squeal about Buster. That's how Joe was. He had no filter. The six–year-old had disappeared into the corner he sat in when he was really in distress, right after vomiting on himself. He rocked quietly and hummed uncontrollably.

"Hey, it's gonna be okay," Jared spoke in a near whisper to his dark-haired little brother. In dirty blue jeans and a dingy vomit stained *Dragon Ball Z* t-shirt, Joe kept his head down as if he didn't hear or see Jared standing in front of him. Jared kicked lightly at his filthy sneaker and said,

"I gotta get rid of the car. I'll be back late. Stay here Joe. Don't leave and don't talk to nobody. Eat some ramen if you get hungry. Two packs are under my bed."

Jared routinely hid food so they'd eat, because Ruth Anne didn't always remember she had kids to feed. He walked out the door and climbed his fourteen years of misery into the driver's seat.

The ashtray was broken off and cigarette butts scattered the floor of the truck. It smelled like Buster, like cigarettes, beer and unwashed fat guy. He never showered. Jared pushed over piles of trash and dirty tools and started the engine. He drove quietly as the sun began to set. Most decent people were finishing up dinner. He was finishing up a crime.

The strong yellow lines along the charcoal highway seemed to guide Jared and he was careful to drive the speed limit so as not to be noticed. He'd driven Buster's truck many times. Mostly to get stuff for Joe or go looking for Ruth Anne in the middle of the night when Buster was sleeping one off, knocked out cold. That night he drove from Lakeland to Bartow and pulled off the side of Highway 98, about one mile from the salvage man's lot surrounded by a chain link fence. He knew that the shop was about to close because he'd gone there often to cash-in scraps of junk cars for money with Jeb, the guy who lived with them before Buster.

The owner of the salvage yard was greedy and ruthless. Jared had seen him steal and cheat customers before. He had no doubt that the old man would take the car and neither ask nor answer any questions, because he'd hardly be willing to rat himself out for stealing Buster's truck. Joe turned off the ignition and threw the key ring with its two keys on the dashboard. He opened the door and climbed down from the old truck. He thought about wiping his finger prints off of the truck but decided not to. Hitting the paved road he turned back in the direction of home and started to walk.

It was close to 7 o'clock and he had twelve miles to go to get back to the trailer and Joe. He didn't risk hitch hiking, because it was dangerous with all the freaks and weirdoes out, but also because he didn't want anyone to relate him to the dead man's truck. He knew it would be way past midnight by the time he got home so he walked as close to the grassy patch beside the road as possible.

Tears came as a surprise. Jared cried for his pitiful, helpless mother. He cried for his brother, who was doomed before he was born. But mostly, he cried for himself. He cried for the little boy who never was.

Chapter 30

....

That was a long time ago. It was the last time Jared ever cried. He was someone else now. Perhaps he was someone just as broken but cracked and shattered in different places. But Jared felt victorious over his past. He felt he had fought the devil and won. Now he had a beautiful wife. Soon they'd have a son.

When René's doctor said the baby was a boy, Jared made up his mind that this son of his would have it all. This boy would have the advantages of the black middle class pedigree and white privilege too. He would be loved and Jared would protect him from all the pain the world had to bring. His son would be all that he couldn't be and never get screwed over the way he had. He'd have so much money, that race, nor anything else would matter. René would love him then. She'd get beyond her daddy and her world of church, clubs, scholarship balls and service projects. She'd finally see him. If she didn't, he was prepared to take his son and go and nobody would stop him, not even high and mighty perfect Pam. He hated his mother-in-law and he knew she thought he was white trash. Maybe he was.

Jared ground his teeth together and winced away the memories and the bad taste the past left in his mouth. He went into the bathroom and spit into the toilet. Dressed, he placed a carefully written note for his wife on the bed. Jared bent down and gave the little dog a hug and a command to "stay," before closing the bedroom door. He walked purposefully to his black BMW and tried to brace himself for what was to come. Ella Jean would be in Annapolis by now and everybody would be rallying around Michelle. He was glad he had the conference in Charleston and decided to continue with his plans as if the accident hadn't happened.

Driving down interstate 50, he thought of René and how he'd keep this thing with Michelle from her. He'd find a way to squash it. Last night on the phone, he'd told her he had a surprise for her. She'd be in later in the afternoon. Sheba was their dog now; Jared would get her back to Michelle when and if the time came. He'd figure something out. He'd find a way to make Michelle understand it had to be done or he'd lie and say Sheba ran away or got hit by a car. Hell, he'd buy another one if he needed to. Every damn body would have a little white toy dog when this was over. The drive to Charleston would give him time to think. He had five hours to come up with a lie and a plan. Jared would have it all figured out by the time he arrived at the conference.

He'd told René he needed to be there a little earlier to brief one of the Division Chiefs. She believed him. She always did. She was easy to lie to. He thought about Michelle and the accident and decided calling the hospital was out of the question. Maybe he'd stop by and pay Michelle a little visit on his way out of town. The easy listening white noise on the radio was the perfect backdrop for his thoughts as he sped along the highway.

Jared figured that once he got the next two payoffs he'd be ready to make a move. His plan was to get out of the navy and leave the country. He already had close to $4,000,000 in his offshore bank account. The next two sales would seal the deal. He knew Michelle's ignorant ass mother was probably swarming around, her but would never figure out what was really going on. He'd call Tony and figure out a way to find out what they knew. Maybe he would say he was checking on her because she was René's cousin. He knew he had to be careful.

Tony Green was his friend and the reason Michelle came on to him in the first place. He and Tony had met in ROTC in Orlando at the University of Central Florida. Tony had done his obligatory five years in the navy and gone on to med school. He was dirt poor and when they met, it was poverty that bound them together. His father died and left his mother and Tony's little brother nothing but debt. He didn't even have life insurance; Captain Hamilton and Pam paid for the funeral. Poverty was new to him but it wasn't new to Jared. So when they met at school, neither of them had all the extra cash and cars that most of the other guys had. It was impossible to date without money. Tony sent every dime he could from his meager ROTC check home to help his mother. Jared saved every penny too. So they developed a brotherhood of poverty.

That was a lifetime ago, long before Tony dated Jared's wife. Now he was in the middle of this mess with Michelle. Both René and Michelle thought he was taking another assignment, but he wasn't. He'd lied to Michelle to he didn't give a shit. He lied to René because he had to.   The plan was in place and the timing was perfect. Leave the navy and move away. He and René could be happy if he could get her away from her controlling family. He'd sell her on the idea of moving out of the country for their son, raising him away from the racism in the good old US of A. She'd buy it. He knew she would.

She would never find out about Michelle. He'd see to that. And the money was going to be an inheritance after he got a convenient letter informing him of the untimely death of his saintly parents. She wouldn't have to know how much it was. He wasn't going to get caught. He'd been so careful these past three years.

When he was first approached about selling military secrets, he'd hesitated. With his security clearance and being connected to soon to-be-Admiral Randolph Hamilton, he definitely had access to what they wanted to know. Jared didn't see himself as a traitor, at first. But you never know what will motivate you to abandon all of your principles.

One night they attended a Boulé Carter G. Woodson lecture series event. He was prepared for a boring night at a table full of black people who thought themselves better than everyone in the universe. This would be business as usual. What he wasn't prepared for was René's reaction to the guest speaker.

At the podium was some guy out of New York that she knew from working in the city. They'd worked together on some 501k. He had a net worth of 5 million and when the lecture was over they'd all gone out for drinks. René seemed captivated and he talked to her as if Jared wasn't sitting right next to her, as if she wasn't wearing his ring. At that moment Jared decided that in order to keep her, he was going to have to be something other than a handsome blond naval officer. All his novelty wore off right then and there, and he felt like his carriage had turned into a pumpkin. Jared saw what he thought was himself in his wife's eyes and he didn't like the image staring back at him.

That night everything changed. He'd agreed to sell Russian operatives the information they wanted. Jared had met his guy on six different occasions and his conscience no longer bothered him. He loved his country but he loved himself more. It was that simple. The first time had been at their wedding reception and the last time was right before getting into the accident with Michelle. There was to be a payoff at Randolph's Change of Command Ceremony in December. He had a few months to get the information he needed to make the sale and then it would be done.

Damn, he thought, *he deserved this*. He'd been crapped on from the start and now he was lifting *himself* as he climbed. He was so close, he could taste it. He and René were going to have a son and nothing was going to stop him from complete execution of the plan, especially not Michelle Washington.

The love of money is the root of all evil.

Chapter 31

....

Pam thanked Reverend Franklin for calling and hung up the phone. Even though she had known him all her life she never addressed him by his first name. The fact that he was in Annapolis and calling her from his cell phone about *her* niece angered her. She shook her head in frustration as she dialed Ella Jean's cell phone number.

"Hello. Ella Jean, what happened? What is going on? How is Michelle? I just got a call from Reverend Franklin. Why didn't you call me? Why am I hearing this from him instead of you?"

"Pam, she gonna be fine. She was driving last night and got banged up pretty bad. She isn't talkin' so much right now but they got her pretty stabilized. Missy don't remember much and she's on a lot of pain medicine. She's got a broken rib and her liver is almost sliced in two. I was going to call you. The hospital called me last night and we drove most of the night to get here. Pam, I'm just tired and I didn't want to worry you. I know Randolph has orders to Norfolk and y'all is trying to pack up."

Ella Jean spoke calmly to her younger sister, trying to remove both fear and fatigue from her voice. She didn't know what she would do if she lost Michelle. Michelle was all she had in the world. She was her life. Michelle was the remnant of sweetness remaining from the horror that was her monster father, Michael Montgomery. Ella Jean knew her daughter wasn't perfect. *How could she be perfect with his DNA?*

"I'm coming to the hospital now. You are being ridiculous. I am not that scared little girl hiding in the closets from mama's belts and her drunken rage. We are grown and we are all we have. It's just us, Ella Jean, and I want to be there for you. The packers are coming this week but family comes first. Always," Pam said, firmly.

She felt that her sister was hanging on by a thread. Michelle had been one disappointment after another and her sweet sister simply didn't deserve Michelle's behavior. The way she talked to her was disrespectful and embarrassing and her careless morals were hard for Ella Jean to take, and even more difficult to watch. Michelle had three abortions in college and she'd been arrested twice for drunk driving and hospitalized once for taking some kind of ecstasy pill at a frat party.

Pam had helped her sister with money and been a listening ear but she wished she could have been more. She'd tried talking to Michelle once before she graduated college. It was to no avail. Her errant niece had promptly told her to mind her own business and reminded her that she was "good and grown." With pursed lips and the snap of her fingers, she'd added that she could do whatever she "damn well pleased." Pam hadn't expected that reaction. Her girls had never talked to her that way. She was saddened and decided to back off and just focus on being there for Ella Jean.

Since finishing graduate school and working as a department manager for the Howard County Medical Research Center, Michelle seemed to have cleaned herself up and appeared to be doing better, but she'd put Ella Jean through way too much. After a mother like Jean, Ella Jean deserved some happiness. What Pam wanted more than anything was for Ella Jean to finally marry Reverend Franklin and let him apply some love to the pain of her past. He was a good man and she didn't understand what was keeping them apart.

It seemed that everyone, except for Ella Jean, could see that he loved her. But it was as if her sister had closed herself off to the possibility of romantic love. After Michelle was born, Pam never saw Ella Jean with any man. She took care of her daughter, went to church every Sunday and went to work at church every day except for Saturday. That was it. That was her routine and her life; church and Michelle.

Pam thought years ago that it was because of Michelle's father. She thought that Ella Jean might still be in love with him. But Ella Jean would never say who he was. She just came home from school that second year, with a belly full of baby and no explanation. She wouldn't talk to anyone about any of it. Pam and Daddy Sloane tried everything. Jean cussed her, yelled and screamed, calling her all kinds of sluts and whores until Daddy Sloane finally put a stop to it. Pam could hear him as if it were yesterday and not all those years ago.

"Jean, there ain't no perfect person, can't you see the girl is hurting? You don't know what happened. Let's not kick her when she's down, especially not you. You're her mother; act like it. She don't have nobody else but us, give her some time and she'll talk when she's ready to talk." His voice was calm and compassionate in contrast to Jean's shrill hateful one. Pam loved him for that.

"That dumb ass piece of shit ain't never gonna amount to nothin' Sloane. You just wastin' money with both of them girls. They spoiled as hell and ain't gonna amount to shit."

Those were Jean's final words on the subject, her final decree on their lives. She would die exactly two years to the day of cirrhosis of the liver. But those were her last harsh words predicting their doom. Pam smiled knowing her mother had died wrong about both she and Ella Jean. She didn't live to see it but that didn't matter. She was wrong. Jean had stumbled off to her room with her dearest friend, Jack Daniels in tow. The bottle was full. The words hurt and Pam just sat in the tiny living room pretending to watch the Ed Sullivan show. A man was juggling while telling jokes. Ella Jean just cried. She cried for what seemed like days, then weeks, then months. No talking, just tears.

"A kind word is sweeter than a honeycomb"

Chapter 32

....

Nobody ever said another word to Ella Jean about being pregnant even though many questions hung in the air like dark shadows. Jean stopped cussing and went back to ignoring both of her daughters and Daddy Sloane got things ready for the baby.

He took Ella Jean to the doctor and got her the prenatal vitamins she needed. She was in her seventh month but he reasoned something was better than nothing at all. In anticipation of new life, Sloane bought a second- hand crib and changing table and painted Ella Jean's room bright yellow. Finally, he loaded his truck with diapers and baby formula and stacked the boxes neatly in the shed towards the back of the house. Ella Jean lay in her small bed and cried until the baby came. She only got up to go to the bathroom or when Daddy Sloane and Pam forced her to eat something. Michelle was incubated on sorrow and regret.

Pam was in the 12th grade and spent her senior year helping Ella Jean put her life back together and take care of her new baby girl. She was afraid of what would happen if she went off to college, so she spent her first year commuting to the junior college. Pam wondered why they changed the name to community colleges. It seemed everything had to always be called something else in the name of progress. She thought about how time tempered Jean and to everyone's surprise, she actually seemed to love Michelle. Baby Michelle was the first person that wasn't a grown man that Pam ever saw her show kindness to. Michelle called her *"momma"* and she let her. Maybe that was progress because Pam and Ella Jean had both been beaten and pinched for calling her anything close to that. It was Jean, just Jean.

Ella Jean started going to the little church down the road every Sunday. Then Sunday's increased to Wednesday night bible study and prayer meeting and Thursday choir rehearsal. She didn't talk a lot but she seemed to be coming back. Around that time, the pastor's wife died in childbirth. Ella Jean seemed to feel so much pain for him and added herself to the list of church members that rotated bringing meals and helped to take care of his new baby boy, Frankie Bea.

Frankie Bea and Michelle grew up together like brother and sister. Eventually, Ella Jean took the job as the church secretary and seemed to find some peace. She was working and she and Reverend Franklin began a lifelong plus friendship. He'd asked her to marry him on two occasions. She said no both times, and he stopped asking, but he never stopped hoping and praying.

Frankie Bea was a good son and worked hard to obey and please his father. He was a motherless child mothered by every girl and woman in the church. But this was not the case with Michelle. Even as a little girl she was rude to Ella Jean and treated her more like an enemy than her mother. Ella Jean never seemed to notice. She just loved her and worked hard to give her everything she needed.

Michelle was five the summer Pam passed Ella Jean's bedroom and overheard the innocent mother and daughter exchange.

"Why come I don't have a daddy like everyone else?" Michelle asked with penetrating seriousness.

"Well Frankie Bea don't have a mother, so sometimes it's just like that, honey." Ella Jean tried to soothe her daughter.

"So did he go to heaven like Frankie Bea's mama?"

Ella Jean hesitated and Pam wondered why. Who was he and was he really dead? What Pam didn't know was that in her hesitation, Ella Jean thought about the devil that repeatedly raped and tortured her. He nearly destroyed her life. Was he in heaven? As far as she knew, he was still very much alive and still stalking prey.

"Yes, baby. Your daddy is in heaven with Frankie Bea's mother and he loved you very much," Ella Jean lied.

Pam left the hallway that day with questions that have never been answered. But Ella Jean knew that Dr. Michael Montgomery hadn't ever laid eyes on his daughter nor had he intended to. Although Michelle never asked again, she seemed to pull even farther away from Ella Jean.

Once Michelle grew up, Ella Jean acted as if it was not strange at all that she had never been to her daughter's house. Every time she tried to visit, Michelle made an excuse about work and not being home. When Thanksgiving, Christmas,

Easter and Mother's Day came, Michelle sent a card but never came home to Mississippi to visit her mother. If Pam and Randolph hosted a big family holiday celebration, Michelle would show up just to spite Ella Jean. It was as if she was saying, *if Pam was my mother, I might actually care.* Pam took to hosting big family gatherings and inviting everyone just so Ella Jean got to spend the holidays with Michelle. She couldn't decide if Michelle was punishing Ella Jean for the circumstances surrounding her birth or if she just simply hated her mother.

Helpless in the hospital, maybe now Michelle would accept her mother's love. Maybe now she'd appreciate all that Ella Jean had sacrificed for her regardless of the circumstances of her birth.

"Pam, I'm sorry," Ella Jean spoke quietly after a long pause.

Pam snapped out of her thoughts about the past.

"I'm here for you, honey. I'm coming to you in fifteen minutes as soon as Rae gets home from work. We're going to go by the hospital first and then we'll come to the house. Do you need me to bring you anything?"

"Pam, I know you're busy, I jest don't want to be a lot of trouble but Pam....I'm scared. I saw a dead bird at her back door." Ella Jean's voice was barely a whisper.

Pam hesitated, wondering if she should mention the dreams. She decided this was not the time. Her sister spoke up as if she was trying to convince herself of something.

"But it's going to be fine though and I'm not leaving her house until she comes home." Ella Jean's determination was evident.

"I'll be there tonight. We are all we have. Forget about the dead bird. It means nothing. Forget the superstitions, Ella Jean. You've been seeing them since you were in college. It's fine. We'll get through this together." Pam winced at the harsh reality that had been and was now their life.

In our weakness his strength is made perfect.

Chapter 33

....

Hanging up the phone she went to the bathroom for her pills. The dreams were occurring with more frequency and they were getting worse. She always woke up in a cold sweat, exhausted. Pam didn't have time for nightmares. She knew lots of kids had rocky starts. But she was determined not to let her memories or the damage of her mother's neglect and hateful treatment disrupt her life, at least not while she was awake.

Rae was scheduled to be home from her summer internship in fifteen minutes. The two of them would go to the hospital and see Michelle and then check on Ella Jean. Pam moved wearily towards the phone, stooping to rest on a box marked "kitchen" packed for Virginia. As the dial tone sounded, she wondered just how many moving parts life could contain. René's soft voice interrupted her worries.

"Hey mom, what a surprise?"

"Listen, your cousin Michelle has been hurt in a car accident. Can you get the girls on so I can fill you all in at one time?"

"Sure," Pam heard a distinct beep as Rachel connected and a second one a few minutes later as Reagan patched in from her car's speakerphone.

"Hey y'all, I'm on the Beltway and these fools are driving crazy fast. What's up?" Reagan bellowed.

"I'm here, still at the office, what a pleasant surprise. Is everybody on here? Dad, Rae?" Rachel queried.

Pam began,

"No, Dad is at a special Plebe Summer, Forestall Lecture and I'll talk to him about all of this later on tonight. Rae is at work and should be home in a few minutes. I'm calling because Michelle has been in a terrible car accident." Pam paused, allowing the girls' time to react.

"I'm going to check on her and to see about your Aunt Ella Jean. Rae and I are driving to the hospital as soon as she gets home."

René spoke first:

"Mom, I'm so sorry. What happened? When I called Jared before going to bed last night, he mentioned hearing about a horrible head-on collision on West Street. He asked if I'd heard anything. Apparently, there was a radio broadcast. He said it sounded awful and he hoped no one got hurt. I would have never in a million years thought it could be Michelle."

"It didn't make the morning paper, probably too late," Pam mused.

"So are you back from New York? When did you get back in town?" Rachel asked.

"I got in this afternoon and my sweet husband left me the most adorable gift before leaving for his conference this morning."

"Come on, Jared! He better be that romantic husband. What was it?" Reagan exclaimed, honking her horn at the guy who just cut her off.

"It was something I've always wanted. It is the most adorable little puppy. He got her just for me, from the pet store in Gambrills. He said he special ordered her about a month ago and she just arrived. She's adorable!"

Pam smiled.

"That's nice honey, perfect timing because he's going to be away for about a week at the Naval Nuclear Power Command at Joint Base Charleston, right?"

The ever practical Pam entered the conversation glossing over the direction it had taken. She couldn't help but wonder how the three girls went from their cousin being in the hospital to René getting a new puppy. She explained that she was signing off and hearing Rae's engine in the front of the house, Pam promised to keep them posted and hung up the phone. The girls stayed on the call to talk about the new dog and Michelle's accident.

Rae and Pam drove in silence to Annapolis Community Hospital. The elevator ride was long and Pam hoped that Rae would be soothing in the hospital room. Not knowing what to expect, she didn't want her youngest daughter's crassness to upset Michelle and make things worse than they were. As they entered the dark room, Michelle lay still on the hospital bed. She was asleep. Rae sat down in the chair and Pam stood over her niece and rubbed the hand without tubes dangling from it. They stayed like that for about thirty minutes. Michelle drifted in and out of consciousness.

"Sheba. Where's Sheba?" You could hear the pain in her voice.

"Shhh, don't try and talk." Pam rubbed her leg beneath the thin hospital blanket.

"It will be alright. Don't worry." She motioned to Rae that it was time to go.

They headed to the door to leave the dimly lit room as quietly as they had come in, to make their way to Michelle's house to see Ella Jean. Pam was thankful that Rae had been silent and subdued in the hospital room. She was in no mood for philosophical rants or probing questions. As they closed the door behind them, Michelle began to moan softly. She sounded so pitiful. Pam couldn't make out what she was saying and continued to walk down the sterile fluorescent hallway. But Rae heard two names clearly.

"Sheba? Sheba? Jared? Where's Jared?"

Chapter 34

....

Summer was at its peak and the hot stickiness only made Pam feel more stuck in the mire of Ella Jean and Michelle. Things seemed to just get worse. The sun was setting, creating a canvas of purples and oranges across the sky as Pam drove to her sister through blinding tears.

"Don't cry, mom. It's going to be alright. Cousin Michelle is a fighter, if she's nothing else. She'll beat this. She's gonna be fine."

Rae tried to reassure her mother, staring at her soft graceful profile as they sped along Spa Road. Pam dabbed at her face with her fingertips in an effort not to disturb her eye makeup. They drove in silence until Rae spoke again.

"Mom, who's Sheba? Was that the person she was going to see when she crashed?"

"I don't know. All the details are sketchy at this point but Reverend Franklin said Michelle was alone and she was on her way home."

Rae hesitated and then decided she needed to ask.

"Mom, are René and Jared close to Michelle? Do they hang out? I didn't think they did, but..." Her voice trailed off.

"No. Unfortunately René doesn't care for Michelle. She says she doesn't like her values but I think it has something to do with Tony Green because I noticed the cooling off around the time all three of them were in Atlanta. Why do you ask, Rae?"

Pam didn't have the patience for any foolishness tonight. She hoped Rae would stop talking about things that weren't pertinent to *right now*. Her cousin was badly injured and that was the focus, not her character or her relationships. She let out a heavy sigh.

"It's nothing. I was just wondering," Rae lied.

They parked the car in Michelle's visitor's parking space and headed to her ground floor condo.

Ella Jean opened the door looking worn out and just tired. She was happy to see both her sister and her youngest niece. Pam always looked good but today she was that *balm in Gilead*. In black Cole Hahn loafers, black fitted pants and a taupe cotton tunic, she looked much younger than her fifty-five years. Ella Jean admired her silver hoop earrings and matching belt as she rushed into the room. Pam always knew what to wear, what to say and what to do.

"Oh Ella Jean, how are you?"

They hugged for a long time. Rae closed the door and moved toward the family room. This was her first time at Michelle's place and everything looked just as she thought it would. There was lots of stainless steel, white leather and glass. The sisters followed her into the kitchen that Michelle clearly never used.

"I know she gonna be alright, Pammy, but I just got a bad feeling about the whole thing. She kept talking about a dog, Sheba. But the doctors say she was alone in that car. Nobody ain't seen no dog."

"Did you say Sheba?" Rae perked up in full investigative mode.

Pam shot her a look that said mind your own business. She didn't speak further about the dog.

"Yeah, that's right." Ella Jean looked inquisitively at Rae whose eyes avoided her aunt's gaze.

"I thought she was delirious at first but then when I got here, I saw the dog bowls in the corner." She motioned to the fancy stainless steel bowls.

"Looks like Missy do have a dog."

Before anyone could say anything the Reverend and his son returned with the groceries. Ella Jean motioned to Rae to get the door. So she let them in and they each greeted her with a nod as they walked passed to place two bags on the kitchen counter.

"Ella Jean, I brought you some extras because I don't want you needing stuff and having no way to get to the store. Pam wondered if he thought she couldn't or wouldn't transport her sister anywhere she needed to go. But then she dismissed the thought as petty. He just wanted to take care of Ella Jean and was very used to it being just the two of them in Pascagoula. The three of them began unpacking the bags of groceries in silence, placing things in the empty cupboards and refrigerator.

Frankie Bea, in jeans and a generic navy blue polo shirt, walked around the kitchen looking at refrigerator magnets and examining pictures. There were two framed museum posters. One about jazz and the other some blues festival. He saw the dog bowls in the corner and opened two of the lower cabinets closest to the bowls. Empty. Then he opened the door to the broom closet. Everybody was busy putting away groceries, each consumed with their own worries. Rae stood in the corner taking it all in. The broom closet had what he'd been searching for. There was a broom, a mop, a bucket and a 10 lb. bag of dry organic dog food. There is or was a dog. Sheba.

Frankie Bea closed the broom closet and headed into the living room to sit on Michelle's massive white leather sofa. There were gray silk pillows and a grey marble coffee table that felt cool to his hand. Her carpet was white. Rae entered the room to catch him holding one of the gray silk pillows to his face and inhaling with his eyes closed. She pretended not to have seen it and he quickly put the pillow down and smoothed it out lovingly. She made herself comfortable on the matching white leather chair directly across from Frankie Bea.

"So we've never met, I'm Rae."

The white leather club chair felt cool on her bare legs. She tugged at the ends of the black cotton dress she'd worn to work and wished she'd had time to change into a pair of jeans.

"Nice to meet you Rae, most folks call me Frankie Bea or Junior. I've heard a lot about your mama and you and your sisters from my dad. Your mama and Miss Ella Jean have known me and my dad since I was born. Shoot, probably before then. They both were like second mothers to me. So it's good to finally put a face with the name."

His eyes darted around the room looking at the sleek silver sculptures and pictures of large white gladiolas on the walls approvingly.

"So are you and Michelle good friends?" Rae questioned the distracted man wondering why anyone would have white shag carpet and how Michelle kept it clean.

"We used to be," Frankie Bea answered with weariness in his voice.

Rae decided she liked this huge dark man with the honest face and chose not to speak but to just listen.

"When we were kids, Michelle and I did everything together. When we were real little we even took baths together," he chuckled at the thought of that.

"You see, Miss Ella Jean worked at the church and since *my* mama died when I was born, she was like the mama I didn't have. Michelle didn't have a father and I like to think my dad was kind of a father figure for her for a while too." Rae smiled and nodded in response to Frankie Bea's memories.

"I took Michelle to the junior and senior prom." Lifting one thigh, he reached into his back pants pocket and pulled out a weathered, brown wallet.

"Here, I got the pictures right here."

He handed the wallet to Rae stretching his huge arm across the coffee table. Staring at the old pictures of two grinning people wearing matching powder blue ensembles in one picture and canary yellow in the other, she didn't recognize Michelle. She looked so happy. Rae handed the wallet back to Frankie Bea and smiled. This was a side of Michelle she didn't know. She wanted to hear more.

Just then, she heard her mother saying her goodbyes to Reverend Franklin and Aunt Ella Jean. Rae jumped up and Pam stuck her head in the doorway of the living room.

"See you next time, Frankie Bea. Give me a hug." Rae watched as the large man got up and walked to the doorway and nearly picked her mother up off the ground in his embrace.

"Rae, come on kiddo, let's let your Aunt Ella Jean and these folks get some rest because Reverend Franklin and Frankie Bea have to get on the road to head back home tomorrow and Ella needs to sleep." She kissed her sister at the door and patted her soft round back, promising to call first thing in the morning.

Chapter 35

….

René sat in the doctor's waiting room flipping the pages of the Fortune magazine. The walls and the vinyl chairs were the same shade of pale blue. Even the carpet underfoot was the same hue. It had been a week since her mother's call letting her know that Michelle was in the hospital. René intended to stop by and visit after her prenatal checkup. Rachel told her that Tony Green was coming over from Walter Reed Army Hospital to take a look at Michelle sometime today. Things didn't look good. She sure hoped their paths didn't cross and had a good mind not to go just because of that.

The nurse came in and called politely,

"René Hamilton-Reed?"

René put the magazine back on the table in front of her and used her hand to lift off from the vinyl covered chair, the squishing sound amplified by the nearly empty waiting room. She walked into the examining room and the door closed behind them. The nurse, who looked too young to even be out of high school took her vital signs and asked her to get on the scale. With all of this done, she undressed and waited for the doctor.

So much had happened since last week. Jared was back home from Charleston and Michelle was still in the hospital. She had taken a turn for the worst. Her liver was severed, and the surgery had not gone as they expected. René was scared for Michelle. The doctors upgraded her condition

from guarded to critical last night. She was proud of Jared because he seemed genuinely concerned and he never seemed empathic to others. He was always so detached. She was glad he'd asked repeatedly about Michelle and her condition. Maybe he was growing spiritually.

Dr. Walker smiled with his whole face when he opened the door.

"How's my favorite mommy-to-be?" The wrinkles in his face hid his blue eyes when he smiled.

"I'm tired," René frowned.

"Well, it comes with the territory. You're about thirty four weeks along and we've got ten weeks or so to go and it'll all be done with. That baby boy will be here!"

He was always cheerful and kind and had known both of her parents for many years spanning many shared military duty stations. René felt safe with him even though her pregnancy was high-risk. She knew she was taking a big chance trying to have a baby, but Jared wanted a baby and their marriage *needed* a baby. It needed some glue and a baby was the best "glue" in René's opinion.

She stretched out as he began to rub the probe over her belly, slathered in cold sticky gel. The faint heartbeat calmed her and the gray and white fuzzy ultra sound images made her baby's life a reality. They were going to have a son. Jared wanted to make him a junior and she wanted to name him after her father, Randolph Michael Hamilton II. They had time to decide.

"Okay, you can get dressed now, René. Everything looks fine, considering your condition."

Dr. Walker went over to the thin desktop monitor and started to type. He thought about the dangers of someone with René's heath issues trying to carry a baby to term and chose his words carefully.

"I want you to take it easy. I'm recommending bed rest for the last stretch. There is too much pressure on your cervix and abdominal floor and I'm concerned about your glucose levels."

René sat up, legs dangling and looked at her shiny red toenails. Jared loved the color red. She thought about all that had to be done at work and the nursery that still needed painting and clothes that needed sorting. How could she just go to bed? Ever since she was a teenager, she'd dealt with doctors, needles and tests. She was diagnosed with fibroid tumors and a retroverted uterus during her first pelvic exam after starting her period and experiencing chronic pain. Now that she was pregnant she had developed gestational diabetes. René didn't care, it didn't scare her and it wouldn't deter her from doing what had to be done to get ready for her son. She whispered a prayer of forgiveness in advance and answered Doctor Walker with her sweetest smile.

"Okay. I will," she lied.

"I'll see you in two weeks, okay?" Dr. Walker patted her shoulder and left her to get dressed.

René' made her way to her parked car and headed for the hospital. She needed to see Michelle because it was the right thing to do, regardless of how she felt about her cousin. She felt guilty because she'd only visited her in the hospital once since the accident and hadn't found time to stop by Michelle's house at all. But Aunt Ella Jean was never there any way because she was spending every waking moment at the hospital. She was practically sleeping there.

René's cell phone vibrated on the passenger seat.

"Hi Mom, what's up?"

René hoped this wasn't going to be a conversation about the danger she'd put herself in by getting pregnant. She didn't have it to give today, no fight left.

Pam chose her words carefully. Thoughts raced through her head. How could this be? This was the call she dreaded and she'd saved it for last. Even though Rae was the youngest, René was the most vulnerable at this point. She was like a porcelain doll and Pam wanted to be careful not to break her.

"René, Michelle is dead."

Chapter 36

. . . .

Ella Jean stood close to her silent daughter, squeezing the lifeless hand that was limp at her side. All the doctor had said was, "I'm sorry." After the frantic screams of "code blue" and what seemed like a thousand resuscitation attempts, he simply said he was sorry. The nurses pulled the tubes from her hands and wrists as if setting her free. Even though it was seven in the morning, the room seemed as dark as if it were midnight to Ella Jean.

The last nurse placed her hand on the sheet and thin blanket resting on Michelle's breast as if she was about to cover her head and face. Ella Jean began to groan.

"Give me some time alone with her."

She spoke to the petite woman who darted around like an apologetic little field mouse. As the small nurse quietly moved toward the door, Ella Jean handed her a card that she kept in the outside pocket of her purse. The card read:

Pamela Sloane Hamilton
410 239-8753

"Call my sister." The words escaped in a hoarse whisper.

The door closed and she was alone in the dark room with the daughter she loved more than life itself. The tears began to well up from somewhere deep and locked inside. Ella Jean lifted Michelle's head and torso. She was stiff and heavy. She sat down on the pillow and rested her daughter's head and upper body on her chest, wrapped both of her ample arms around her child's shoulders and held on tight. Michelle's eyes were closed and she still felt warm. She looked peaceful in an eerie kind of way. Rocking back and forth, Ella Jean let out a wail like a banshee in the dark of night. It was a wail designed to wake the dead, except it didn't. So she wailed some more. She moaned and she cried.

Pam marched down the hospital corridor at a clipped pace. This wasn't supposed to be happening. Pam mentally repeated over and over, that Michelle was dead, to prepare herself for opening the hospital room door. She had dreamed of vultures and bats eating the flesh of a sparrow last night. The sparrow had the face of a woman. She woke up frantic and sweating and couldn't go back to sleep. She didn't risk trying to take pills because she knew Randolph was awake even though he was still and didn't make a sound. She didn't trust herself with the doors to the drawers in the bathroom and couldn't risk the questions. So she just reclined there, staring at the ceiling by the lines of light peeking in through the blinds. She'd been up since three in the morning.

Randolph got up at six like he did every morning and got dressed to go for a run.

"Sweetie, you didn't get much sleep did you?" He stroked the side of her face with his hand.

"No, I didn't but I'm okay. I just had a bad dream." That was all she could think to say, pulling his hand to her mouth and kissing the back of it.

"You want some eggs and bacon?" Her smile was weak and tired.

"Only if you feel up to it and only if you're cooking for yourself. I can just have some fruit and coffee, Pam. Don't go through any trouble for me. Please."

Pam turned on the shower and waited for the front door to close. She reached into the back of the top vanity drawer and found the magic that would get rid of the anxiety she felt. She swallowed three tiny yellow pills with spit and got into the shower.

With her husband back from his run, the morning had started off like most mornings. It was the most natural thing in the world for her to share the newspaper with Randolph over a sunny side up egg and one slice of bacon. Randolph had whole wheat toast, she had some melon or fruit. It was comfortable and natural, a ritual they had repeated for over thirty years. Once in his uniform, Randolph prepared to walk to work, which was one of the perks of being stationed at the Naval Academy. He kissed her cheek and whispered,

"Keep it warm for me."

Pam laughed, "Shoot, I gotta get it warm first, unless you talking about these eggs and this bacon!"

Randolph chuckled and headed out of the kitchen and through the front door. The phone rang and everything changed.

Racing down the hall at Annapolis Medical Center, Pam remembered the pain in the woman's voice when she answered the phone.

"May I speak with Mrs. Pamela Sloane Hamilton?"

"This is she."

"Mrs. Hamilton, I'm calling on behalf of your sister, Miss Ella Jean Washington. She wanted you to know her daughter passed this morning at 7 a.m. If you could come here, that would be good. I don't think she's doing so well herself."

Pam hung up the phone and grabbed her keys and purse.

Michelle dying was the most unnatural thing in the world. Pam could hear her sister wailing and chanting, "*my baby, my baby*" over and over as she got closer to the room. She was not prepared for the pitiful sight waiting for her when she opened the door. Ella Jean was perched on the bed like an eagle protecting her nest, bathed in yellow flowers on her black silky blouse with ruffled bell sleeves and ruffles down the front. The massive flowers framed Michelle's lifeless head like funeral wreaths. Her straight hair was smashed against her mother's breasts and reaching in all directions. Ella Jean squeezed the small brown body in the white hospital gown, wet with a mothers tears and a clear liquid dripping from Michelle's dead lips. Pam couldn't find words.

"Ella Jean, don't..."

She ran to her sister and rubbed up and down her soft shoulder. Ella Jean's face was contorted with pain and drenched in tears and saliva. Her turned down lips parted, and her teeth clenched, she continued to moan and rock.

"I'm here. It's okay. Don't make yourself sick, Ella Jean." Her words sounded stupid, silly even as they escaped her mouth. She had built her whole life around knowing what was appropriate for what occasion. It made her feel secure, and it made life bearable, and often even made the grotesque things pretty. It was her guiding structure. So what did Emily Post say was appropriate for a mother with a broken heart who was facing putting her child in a box and then a hole and covering it with dirt. How could that ever be made pretty? She whispered in her sister's ear:

"I'm sorry, Ella Jean. I'm so sorry."

Chapter 37

….

Ella Jean got through that day and was persuaded by Pam, René and Rae to leave the hospital and let Michelle's body be picked up by the funeral director's transport team. That was two days ago and she hadn't said much since she left the hospital. Reverend Franklin and Frankie Bea arrived late that night and checked in to one of the economy hotels near the Annapolis mall. He was staying to get Ella Jean back to Mississippi safe and sound. Frankie Bea looked broken, as if someone had simply snapped something holding his parts together on the inside.

They sat in Michelle's small condo with René and Rae. Reagan and Rachel were in D.C. but flying down to Pascagoula for the funeral, which if Pam had her way, was going to be at Reverend Franklin's church. In her mind there was no need to prolong this thing and drag it out. It would only prolong Ella Jean's pain. So she and Reverend Franklin took care of all of the arrangements. The only task Ella Jean wouldn't relinquish was choosing what Michelle would wear lying in the open casket.

Ella Jean selected a beautiful cream suit with a straight skirt from Michelle's closet. She chose a cream silk blouse and packed it to take to the funeral parlor. Then she carefully selected a black bra from Michelle's lingerie chest. She didn't want her bra to show through her blouse when mourners were viewing her daughter's body. She couldn't find a slip or stockings and decided she'd pick both up when she got home.

Ella Jean didn't like any of Michelle's panties but no daughter of hers was going to meet Jesus without underwear, so she selected a black stretchy thing that looked like shorts that and said "*Spanx*" on the inside label. It was too stretchy to be a girdle but Ella Jean decided it would be fine. It belonged to Michelle, it matched the bra and it was probably something smart, because her "Missy" was so smart. Tears welled up again but no one talked.

They moved about completing the task before them and doing what needed to be done in the silence of sorrow. Ella Jean's cell phone sat on the sofa and its ringing was a welcomed interruption. Rae answered the phone and went into the bedroom to give it to her aunt. Next to Michelle's bed on her nightstand was a picture of a smiling Michelle and a small white dog. It looked a lot like René's new dog, *Miss Petey*. She handed the phone to her aunt who was going through Michelle's closet, carefully taking clothes out and folding them to take home.

"Your phone was ringing. Aunt Ella Jean, it's the Reverend."

She handed the small phone to Ella Jean and made a mental note to say nothing to anyone about the dog. She was sure her mother already knew, because she'd helped pack up Michelle's things during the past few days. Rae decided to wait. She left the room and left her aunt alone to commune with Reverend Franklin.

In the living room her mother and René were packing up books and pictures, wrapping the paintings and framed posters carefully in paper and bubble wrap as they took them off the wall. Ella Jean wanted all of Michelle's things to be transported to Mississippi and she didn't want strangers to touch them. Pam had taken care of contracting a moving company and they had already dropped off several boxes.

Flowers had come from Michelle's boss and two women from work who said they were her friends had brought a tray of sandwiches by. Ella Jean did not want any of this. She refused to hold these sacred rituals in Maryland. Pam got the sense that if she was going to ever be able to say goodbye, it would have to be on her own terms and at home in Mississippi.

Rae wanted to talk to René about the dog but she also wanted to protect her sister from foolishness. Most of all, she didn't want to piss her mother off. Rae knew that her mother thought she was always inappropriate and intrusive. In her mind she was just upfront, "keeping it real." She chuckled at the corniness of the phrase. Rae thought her mother inevitably looked away from things she needed to face and stare at head on. Pam pretended bad things weren't so bad. But sometimes they really were.

"René, how's Miss Petey doing?"

Rae walked up to her very pregnant sister dressed in tan maternity pants, camel colored leather ballet flats and a cream boat neck cashmere sweater. It was probably not a maternity sweater, just something René got in a large size, because it hugged her belly like a desperate lover as she moved methodically to get the pictures wrapped and sorted.

René decided that she would not tell anyone what Doctor Walker said about bed rest. The baby would be fine. She would take it easy but she couldn't shut it down. Not now. Her mother needed her. Hoping she was not doing their son harm, she pushed away the guilt and fear that loomed right below the surface and directed her attention to Rae's question.

"Oh I love her! She's such a sweetie pie and I'm so glad we got the dog before the baby came. Jared did a good thing."

Pam listened and looked over at Rae trying to subliminally communicate to her to shut up. She knew where this was heading. She'd seen the dog. Her thoughts raced to put out any fires before they started. *So what if Michelle's phantom dog "Sheba" looked like Miss Petey. Was there only one white Maltese in the world? Michelle kept everything about her life cloaked in such secrecy that nobody even knew she had a damn dog.* Pam glared at her youngest daughter but Rae refused to make eye contact and continued with her transparent investigation.

"Whose dog is it really? You know a puppy always has a favorite. Does Miss Petey favor Jared over you?"

René laughed. "Well, Miss Petey loves both of us but she and Jared became fast friends right away. It's almost as if they knew each other in another life. She sleeps on his side of the bed and follows him around when he's home. Jared is such a loner, she's good for him."

Pam spoke up. "Pets are good for the soul. It was thoughtful of Jared to get the dog."

Her smile reflected intense pain right beneath its surface. The dream returned last night and she woke up with yet another pounding headache. That morning, Pam only took ibuprofen; she had to wean herself from the pain meds. If she could just hold on and get Ella Jean through Michelle's funeral and René through this pregnancy, things would get better. Everything would calm down when Randolph took command of SOCOM. She sensed something was brewing with Reagan and Rachel too. She needed to find out what was going on. Then she could focus on herself and put the pieces back together a little better.

"Rae, how about running an errand for me? My keys are in my purse on the table and we need more book boxes."

Pam stared her daughter in the face and dared her to object.

Calling her mom's bluff and determined to find out if her suspicions about her brother-in-law were true, she busied herself with a stack of books and said,

"Mom, the moving company would send those by if we just asked them to. This is a phone call, not a Rae running an errand thing."

Throwing the final trump card, Pam told her daughter that the time it would take was time they didn't have and that it would be less work for everybody if they had the boxes and could finish up. Rae grimaced and silently went to retrieve the keys and head to the moving company's office and warehouse on Admiral Kidd Drive.

Chapter 38

….

The jazz singer's voice going on about birds in the sky and knowing how she felt was a sharp contrast to the atmosphere inside of the black Audi A6. Trent drove through the city headed to Interstate 295 to the airport with Sean in the passenger seat. Clad in a gray lightweight cotton V-neck sweater and black dress shoes, he looked more relaxed than he was. Everything about this situation was tense and difficult. Sean slouched in his seat, tapping his finger to the beat against his jeans. Wearing a tan gingham shirt and loafers he thought about the times he'd seen Michelle and actually talked to her. He felt guilty because he'd never really made any attempt to know her. She always seemed a bit spacey to him and drank too much at every family gathering. Sean caught up with the direction his mind was headed and thought, *"Damn, I'm judging her even now. What kind of asshole does that?"*

Their wives sat in silence in the back seat. Rachel closed her eyes and leaned her head against the seat allowing her Prada sunglasses to hide her wet, red eyes. She couldn't believe Michelle was dead and they were headed to the airport to board a plane to Mobile, Alabama. From Mobile, they'd take the forty-five minute drive over to Pascagoula and bury Michelle. Reagan must have felt her anguish. She squeezed her sister's hand against the cool gray leather upholstery with her long slender fingers.

Rachel opened her eyes and glanced down at her sister's hands and nails and smiled. They were the brightest neon yellow she had ever seen. They matched her yellow skinny jeans and her multicolor striped cotton scarf halter top that exposed parts of her flat stomach and torso. On her feet were orange *Tom's* that were a little frayed from wear. Her appearance was a sharp departure from Rachel's white linen oversized shirt and matching drawstring pants and white low-heeled sandals. Her silver and white bangles and diamond stud earrings served as a contrast to Reagan's gold belly ring and colorful clunky necklace. Rachel loved her sister's boldness and Reagan admired the stability that Rachel brought to any situation. As the car raced down the highway they sat, fingers entwined, listening to the lone voice of the singer on the radio bellowing about *"feeling good."*

Reagan had begun teaching a summer session and had to cancel class for two days. She was sure her students were happy. She thought it odd that no matter what happened in the world, good or bad, it had the opposite effect on somebody somewhere. Michelle's death brought such unexpected sadness but to 32 twenty year olds it was a welcome day off from a summer college course required for their major. It was horrific for Aunt Ella Jean, but perhaps it would be good fortune for Reverend Franklin. Maybe Ella Jean would finally focus her attention on him and the kind of relationship he so desperately wanted.

Letting go of Rachel's hand, she took her phone out of her huge burlap bag and began to text her sister while sitting next to her.

Guess who's pregnant?

Rachel looked at the screen of her phone on her lap and peered over her glasses to check her sister's face.

"NO!!! Why didn't u tell me? Does Sean know? Mom?

Reagan quickly typed.

"I wanted to wait 2 c if God wld let me keep it and no they don't know - I was going 2 tell them both but then poor Michelle so - later When we get back - just passed 3 mos n no blood!!! "

Rachel smiled for the first time in weeks. Trent looked back at them suspiciously in his rear view mirror. He wondered if they thought he and Sean didn't know they were texting each other. His guess was Rachel was telling Reagan that they had finally decided to look into adoption. He had a peace about it and they were both tired of the stress that trying to have a baby had put on their marriage.

They were five minutes from the airport and he thought about his wife and her sister. Even though all four of the Hamilton sisters were close, the two in the back seat were truly best friends. They talked on the phone daily and lunched and gallery hopped together. The four of them had enjoyed many ski trips and weekend jaunts. He hoped the girls knew how much he and Sean respected that and admired their relationship and how much their husbands benefited from their closeness. Sean was an only child and Trent's home had included money, status, adultery and hypocrisy. He thought the Hamilton's were to be commended for their values and the love that was clearly evident in their family.

As they parked the car and made their way to the gate to board the plane, each of the four tried to mentally prepare themselves for Ella Jean's grief. They'd reserved one rental car and no one was looking forward to the dreaded drive from Mobile to Pascagoula.

Rachel broke the silence as the four walked through the corridor to find their seats across the aisle from each other in the front of the plane.

"Mom said Aunt Ella Jean couldn't bear a wake and viewing. So tonight we are just going to go over to the house and sit with her. Dad, Rae and mom are staying at the old house with Ella Jean."

"I always thought a wake and a funeral was like having two funerals," Trent spoke in a calming tone as he stored the two small suitcases in the overhead compartment.

"Me too, Trent, it's like having a two-day funeral," Reagan added as she plopped in her seat, buckled her seatbelt and imagined poor Michelle, cold on a mortician's table.

Trying to provide some levity, Sean chuckled, squeezing his wife's yellow clad thigh.

"You know not to do any of this with me right? When I'm gone, I'm gone. Say a few words, donate my body to some medical school and call it a wrap."

Reagan didn't want to think about it all right now, kissing Sean's cheek she asked across the aisle, "So are René and Jared at the St. George hotel with us?"

"I don't know. I've called and texted her and gotten no response, I'm a little worried. But since there are only three decent hotels, she shouldn't be hard to find."

The strong must bear the infirmities of the weak.

Chapter 39

....

The red brick one-story house sat proudly on the corner lot. The lawn was small but green and free of weeds. Frankie Bea saw to that when he mowed the lawn every week. Rows of colorful petunias lining the short driveway leading up to the front steps were vibrant and inviting. Perched on the top step was a small girl eating a Popsicle. On the porch proper, were two rather large ladies from church. They each sat in green and white metal gliders moving slowly in unison. The air was thick and it was so hot that even the smallest exertion of energy was to be avoided.

Inside, the living room was bursting with mourners. Each of the three chairs and the small sofa was filled. Several people balanced paper plates piled with food on their laps and munched in silence. The small dining room boasted a china cabinet and a table with a starched white table cloth. The six dining room chairs had been commandeered to the living room and lined the wall next to the huge television in a wooden console. The chair cushions were avocado green and covered in clear plastic. The plastic insured that the upholstery would outlast the wood. Pam remembered when Daddy Sloane bought the set when she was in high school. Ella Jean had kept it well. She always took great care of things.

The epicenter of the grief was located in the kitchen. Randolph sat at the small kitchen table talking to Reverend Franklin. Rae and Frankie Bea had gone in his pick-up truck to get more ice and Ella and three deaconesses from church were unwrapping pies and cakes and large platters of baked and fried chicken. They were busy refilling the dishes on the table and putting out more plates. Pam was at the kitchen sink, which was filled with lemons. She systematically rolled each on the counter to loosen the juice to make lemonade. The house hummed with mourning and motion, there was no music playing and the television was off. Ella Jean wore a black cotton dress and black vinyl sandals. She and the deaconesses each donned aprons with the church logo and a cross on the front.

The rental car pulled up to the curb and spilled its reluctant occupants out. The foursome walked up to the porch to enter the house. The ladies on the porch looked at them as if they were celebrities as they often did "folks from up north."

"Hey, how's everybody?" Reagan came up the steps first and entered the house. Rachel and the guys followed. They had come straight from the airport rather than checking in to the hotel first. They spoke to the people in the living room and went into the kitchen. The guys greeted Randolph and eased their way into the conversation with him and Reverend Franklin. Rachel and Reagan found their aunt.

Rachel approached her in the hallway and wrapped her arms around her. She smelled like peaches and nutmeg.

"I'm so sorry, Aunt Ella Jean. I'm so sorry."

"I know, baby. I know. Ain't nothin' we can do now. She in the Lord's hand now." This was Ella Jean's response as she patted Rachel on the small of her back.

"What can we do? What needs to be done?" Reagan chimed in after kissing her soft and tender Aunt Ella Jean. They always loved her and she was always good to them, baking cookies and coming to stay with them when they were little and their mom flew to join their deployed father. She was kind and loving and they had fond memories of rich peach cobbler and delicious pound cakes. The only bad memories were how mean Michelle was some times. She would break their toys, lie about it and she hated to share her stuff. But Aunt Ella Jean had always been the same old Ella Jean.

"Go into my room and look at the funeral program your mom and I worked on. Look it over and take it down to the printer for me and make some copies." Ella Jean pointed the way to her room. The girls went to do as they were asked.

Pam looked out of the tiny window over the sink and thought about her life growing up in that house. Ella Jean saying to her girls, "go into my room" triggered painful memories of the countless times Ella Jean had whispered those words to her as Jean's belt or fist came pounding down on some unsuspecting part of Ella Jean's body. At first, Pam would scurry quickly and crawl under her sister's bed and wait for her to come in bruised and tearful. But as they grew older, Pam stopped running, refusing to obey her sister's command. She decided not to escape from her mother's drunken tirades but rather share the blows with Ella Jean in her own heroic act of solidarity. Even thought they'd both end up locked in the front hall closet until thirty minutes before Daddy Sloane arrived home from work; it was somehow better because it was shared suffering. They were trapped together and Ella Jean told her stories and held her hand in the darkness. She remembered crying herself to sleep and wondering what she could do to make her mother love her and Ella Jean. Ella Jean had the closet door removed and the closet bricked up when Daddy Sloane died, and the house became hers.

Her mother Jean, Daddy Sloane and Ella Jean stayed together and tried to be a family. In spite of everything, there had been some good times. Pam preserved the good times in her mind while staying at Ella's house, she savored those memories and let them linger. The bad memories seemed so distant and buried far away now that Michelle was dead. She thought that this one awful thing was so painful and present that it put some of the past in perspective, somehow softened it.

Pam hadn't had one of those dreadful dreams since she'd been there. It had been three days. Randolph and Rae came last night but before that, she and Ella Jean had simply enjoyed their time together in spite of the circumstances. They'd laughed and cried, remembering their mother's cruel words and punishments and more importantly, their father's undying love.

Even though Michelle was dead, the past few days were good ones for the two sisters. The days were easy starting off with the two of them cooking breakfast together and eating at the little white and gray speckled kitchen table. They ended on the porch gliders with Pam's homemade lemonade in Mason jars. They watched fireflies dance and talked about their choices, their children and their lives. Pam slept in her old room that was now Ella Jean's guest room. It was neat with pink flowers on the wall and a high bed with a quilt of pink floral patterns and brown dolls propped on it.

Michelle's room was Ella Jean's old room and it remained as it was the day of Michelle's high school graduation. Ella Jean cleaned it once a week and washed the bed linen but could not bear to change anything in it. Ella Jean had taken over the master bedroom across from the home's one bathroom. After Daddy Sloane died, she gave the furniture to a lady at church and bought herself a brand new bedroom set. With the walls painted a pretty powder blue and a blue quilt decorated with flowers, she settled into the little house and found peace.

Pam planned to stay for a week to make sure Ella Jean was okay. After that she needed to head to Virginia to get ready for her husband's change of command. Weary of the constant moving, she secretly hoped this would be the last one.

Chapter 40

....

The tiny church smelled of mildew because the carpet was old, and had survived too many floods and there was never enough money to replace it no matter how many fish fries they had or chicken dinners they sold. The stained glass windows were open but there was no breeze, just heat soaking every inch of the small sanctuary. The ten rows of wooden pews were packed with mourners. There were friends of Michelle from college and members of her sorority who had arrived early to perform a time honored moving and private farewell ceremony for their dearly departed Soror. Ella Jean didn't like the fact that she couldn't see what they were doing or hear what they were saying but Pam, who had pledged a different sorority in college, convinced her it was a good thing and would be what Michelle would have wanted.

Among the mourners seated in the pews were a sprinkling of Michelle's high school and elementary school friends and teachers, but mostly there were people who came because of Ella Jean. She was liked and well- respected by the small community because she worked as the church secretary and was so giving. Each member had an "Ella Jean" story about being the recipient of her kindness at one time or another. Sometimes it was in the form of a pound cake, other times it was a visit or a get- well card. There were only a handful of blood relatives because Jean had left home in disgrace long before Ella Jean and Pam were born and Daddy Sloane only had one brother who lived far away in Arkansas.

Reverend Franklin, wearing a long black robe, patted his face with a handkerchief as he sat in the large ornate high backed chair. His chair behind the pulpit was flanked by two smaller chairs designated for assistant ministers. They were both empty because the congregation could barely pay one preacher; assistants weren't in the budget. Behind them stood the choir of five elderly women and men who hadn't known Michelle. Clad in white on top and black on the bottom, they were there for Ella Jean and stood ready to sing the songs of Zion that would usher Michelle's soul into the pearly gates.

Pam sat on the front pew next to her sister in a black sleeveless dress and a black wide brimmed straw hat. Ella Jean was motionless in her black polyester funeral suit that she wore for the many funerals she attended at the little country church on the dirt road. Her massive black funeral hat had a huge veil that hung over her face like so much sorrow. She thought it was the strangest thing that she was wearing her funeral ensemble for her own daughter's home going service. That simply was never supposed to have happened. There was no crying left to do; she was all cried out and the absence of tears was replaced by a quiet resolve that was difficult to understand.

All eyes were drawn to the brightly colored wreath and the blood red spray of roses that draped the white steel casket. The lid was open, revealing Michelle, looking more angelic in death than she had ever appeared in life, arms at her side, lips sealed with mortician's glue. The tiny organist with her floral hat perched on her head began softly playing:

Come, ye disconsolate where'er ye languish, Come to the mercy seat, fervently kneel. Here bring your wounded hearts, here tell your anguish; Earth has no sorrow that heaven cannot cure...

Randolph and Rae sat stoic behind Ella Jean and Pam on the second row. Randolph's black suit was a sharp contrast to his usual uniform with all the ribbons and brass. Today, for Ella Jean, he wanted to be everyman, not superman. It was about her loss, not his brass and he wanted everyone in this small town to be clear about that. From the back of their heads, Rae in black pants and a black linen jacket appeared to be his young son. She sat thinking about Michelle, the little dog, and mostly about Jared.

Next to her was René, pregnant with Jared's son and doubt about the future of her marriage. She was at that funeral in body only. Her thoughts were stuck in her kitchen in Annapolis three nights ago when all hell literally broke loose. It was a typical night, Jared cleared the dinner dishes because she had cooked and then he went to walk the dog. She'd showered and washed her hair and decided to let it air dry. She'd planned to pull the wild curls up into a bun because she was too tired to blow dry and straighten her hair. Slipping down the stairs to get a glass of water and grab her Kindle from the kitchen table, she heard the back door open. Jared knelt down to pet Miss Petey who was blissfully wagging her tail in excitement.

"Good girl, Sheba. You're a good girl." He whispered with his nose nuzzling her face.

But before he could remove her pink leather collar he looked directly at his wife's face as she stood by the refrigerator door holding a glass in one hand and her Kindle in the other.

For a minute neither of them spoke, knowing they had flung a door wide open that they'd hoped to keep locked forever. The one thing that had always been clear but never spoken was that once opened, the door would be impossible to close.

René was the first to speak, "What did you call Miss Petey?"

She moved closer to her husband, her eyes never leaving him. Jared continued to focus on the dog, gave her a little pat and she scampered off to get water. He walked toward his pregnant wife and reached for her arm.

"René, I'm not Tony, I would never…"

The betrayed pregnant woman screamed, "So you know about Tony?"

Pulling her arm away from him and backing herself against the kitchen counter, René sat the glass and Kindle down. She felt flushed with heat, despite wearing only a thin white cotton maternity gown. Perspiration seeped from her wild curly hair to her bare feet.

"Is that Michelle's dog, Jared? Do you not think my whole family is not wondering about this dog? Is that Michelle's dog? Did you give me Michelle's… How? How'd you get the dog? Did you lie to me?! Have you been…?" The questions tumbled out faster than she could think.

Jared stood glued to the floor in his black polo and jeans. His mind raced for words, for an explanation, for a good lie. He was not prepared to tell the truth. But it was too late, his silence answered all of René's questions, spoken and unspoken.

"How could you? Were you sleeping with her, Jared?"

"René, I… I love only you. I love you baby and you know that." He moved closer and words erupted from somewhere in her mind she had never allowed herself to travel.

"Who are you? Who are you Jared? Where are your parents? My sisters were right! Who are you? I know who you are! YOU'RE TRASH! You are *sneaky* poor w…"

The impact of the back of his opened hand on her angry face stunned both of them just as much as it hurt her. Jared was sorry for all of it and so was she. That night she'd locked herself in the guest bedroom and sat up all night with a flood of tears as her sole companion. Feeling utterly alone she prayed and cried. She cried for herself, her husband, her marriage, and their unborn son.

René almost didn't come to the funeral but knew that was not the right thing to do. She had to be there. She needed to see her mother and her father, even if she couldn't talk to them. Sitting in this pew, she was certain her husband had been in a relationship with Michelle and knew more about her accident than he was letting on. He knew about the accident before anyone else did and the dog appeared the day after. He was probably involved. If Michelle was capable of this, what about Tony? Had it been her goal to sleep with every man René ever loved? Silent tears of regret instantly appeared and everyone but Jared thought the tears were for Michelle.

Jared tried to touch his wife's hand in an attempt to soothe her, to stop the flood of tears, to say he was sorry for the hundredth time. René moved her hand in a quick motion that caught the attention of Trent, Rachel, Sean and Reagan sitting next to them. Rae leaned forward and stared into his eyes. She knew guilt when she saw it and what she recognized written all over his face was guilt. On their row, only Randolph seemed to not notice René pull away from her husband because Captain Hamilton kept his mind and eyes fixed on the white box containing Michelle's stiff body.

Jared felt like his pristine white uniform was covered with dirt. He felt soiled and poor and pitiful. He felt like Ruth Anne's son and he hadn't felt that way in many years. He had never meant to hit her. The word trash was some kind of trigger. René was his world and even he didn't understand what happened between him and Michelle. He didn't know why he cheated on his wife and if he could take it all back he would. But he couldn't so he had to fix it.

After Buster, Jared never intended to kill again. But he had to fix it. He had to create a world for René and their son, one of wealth and privilege and he was so close. Michelle was dead and he had come into the hospital and slipped rosiglitazone into her IV on that sweltering night, betting on the fact that Ella Jean would never approve of an autopsy. Her heart just stopped. It was awful and he was truly sorry but it had to be done. She was calling his name and asking about him, sending messages by Tony even.

That night he'd gotten her call and she was doing better and rapidly piecing together the events of the night of the accident. She wanted to know what happened to Sheba. Michelle was furious and threatening to tell René everything and he couldn't have that. She was starting to want more, talking about marriage and him divorcing his wife. That little freak, Rae, was asking questions about the dog. He looked straight ahead and whispered in the direction of the waiting casket,

"I'm sorry."

Those who heard it, including René, thought he was talking to her. He was talking to Michelle and he really was sorry, for all of it. But there was one more person that had to be eliminated. It wasn't personal. Only Buster was personal but this would be the last one and he wouldn't do it himself. Contact had already been made and this could all have been avoided if Jackson had just kept his mouth closed.

Unbeknownst to Jared, two men watched him intently. Staring at the back of his blonde head one row behind him on a pew across the aisle sat Frankie Bea, working out his own feelings of loss and anger. Captain Jackson McDonald sat directly behind Jared, holding his wife Anne's hand. He wondered if Jared knew how much the Navy Inspector General (I.G.) knew about what he'd been doing and if he should tell Randolph everything he'd learned. Knowing only a fraction of Jared's deeds, he thought, *"This little shit. He won't get away with this."* As if reading his mind, Anne placed her hand on top of her husband's, trying to keep his thoughts on the fact that Pam was burying her niece today.

Reverend Franklin took his seat after forty-five minutes of talking about "Sister Michelle's" life and lying about her character. What could be said? It was one of those things that happened at funerals. The elderly choir stood up and sang.

Some bright morning when this life is over
I'll fly away
To that home on God's celestial shore
I'll fly away

I'll fly away, oh glory
I'll fly away in the morning
When I die Hallelujah by and by
I'll fly away I'll fly away…

This signaled the end of the service and the beginning of the recessional. Pam held on to her sister as the quiet funeral service attendants in their black suits donning white gloves closed Michelle up in the rectangular satin lined box and wheeled it down the center aisle. Ella Jean and Pam followed, holding on to each other in complete silence. On the last row, in the far corner, was a frail woman watching everything. She marveled at how Ella Jean had aged. No one noticed her, but Miss Mary had to be there. She slipped out through side door near the little cemetery as the rest of the sanctuary spilled out of the front of the church.

One thing they were both sure of: Michelle would have hated every minute of this service.

The sun was shining bright and the sky was crystal clear when the men and women piled out of the hot church. Folklore has it that a rainy day for a funeral is a sign that the deceased is in heaven and a clear day, that they are in hell with certainty.

Part III

Autumn

The Promise of Power

Chapter 41

.....

Pam and Ella Jean sat on the porch and listened to the chirping birds. Randolph and Rae had driven to the airport earlier after a wonderful breakfast of fried apples, biscuits and pork sausage patties. Even though Rae turned her nose up at the idea of "frying perfectly good fruit" and wouldn't touch the sausage, Pam and Ella Jean could tell she loved the biscuits and apples. Randolph had read the local paper, ate and quietly watched his daughter's antics.

"Y'all got to fry everything? Do you have to make your biscuits with white flour and animal fat?" She'd hissed at her aunt and mother, reporting to the kitchen packed and ready to go to the airport.

"But those smells of good, fried, and baked with lily white flour lured you into dis kitchen didn't they?" Ella Jean chuckled.

"There is a bowl of fruit on the table or dad can get you a spinach and egg white sandwich from the Starbucks at the airport if you don't want to eat what we two sisters of the south have prepared." Pam laughed at her culinary alliance with her sister. She felt better than she had in months.

No fight to be had, Rae sat down and served herself a generous portion of fried apples and consumed two biscuits slathered in butter; white flour and all. Sitting across from her father she sipped fresh squeezed orange juice and enjoyed the breakfast more than she expected to. After hugs, kisses and goodbyes, they were on their way. The others had left last night, and René and Jared headed back to the airport directly after the funeral. René said something about a meeting she needed to prepare for.

The brief time spent with Ella Jean before Michelle's funeral had been good for both she and Pam. Ella Jean was away from the church with company at her house and sitting on the porch had always personified peace for Pam. Ella Jean thought a lot about the life Michelle had lived. Her things would arrive later on in the week and she was going to make room for them in the house until she was ready to part with them. Ella Jean wanted to talk to Pam about something she found that broke her heart but she wanted to wait until after the burial ceremony. Maybe this morning would be the time to talk.

"Pam, Missy had a diary." Ella Jean spoke soft and deliberate.

Pam waited to hear what her sister would say next and felt the peace she'd found threatened. She didn't want to be privy to Michelle's inner thoughts or her life's secrets. But she knew her sister needed her to listen. It was the right thing to do.

"She was not a good person and I'm sorry." Ella Jean looked straight at the horizon as tears began to flow.

"We can't control our kids Ella Jean, they are who they are. They come from us but they *are not us*; they are on loan to us from God. It's okay." Pam didn't know what else to say.

Ella Jean was quiet for a while and when she opened her mouth to speak again, she went on to talk for hours about the contents of the diary. She told stories of abortions, married men and other things that brought them both pain to know. But the thing that brought her unspeakable sorrow was the discovery of her daughter's hatred for her. She couldn't make sense of it.

"Pam, we had a mother who just didn't know how to love us and even we didn't hate her. I gave everything I had to Missy. I don't know how she could hate me."

"Hurt people, hurt people," Pam whispered and continued to glide back and forth on the porch.

She told Ella that people in pain cause more pain. She felt that people couldn't bring to a situation anything beyond what they had and who they were. Michelle had always been broken and unhappy. She reassured Ella Jean over and over again that it simply wasn't her fault.

Ella Jean quietly dropped the bomb that changed the whole morning when she told Pam that the diary also revealed Michelle was sleeping with René's husband and had been for over a year. Ella said they were probably together the night of the accident because the last diary entry was the morning of the crash and it laid out plans for them to meet and go to Charleston. Pam couldn't speak. Her throat was tight and she felt like her head was going to explode.

"No! That's not possible! She wouldn't do that! Jared wouldn't do that!" She was firm in her assertions and stared at her sister in complete disbelief.

"I'm sorry," was Ella Jean's only reply.

Pam didn't know what to do with any of this. If she told Randolph, he'd kill Jared. Period. She could tell René. What if she didn't even suspect anything? Pam decided to pray about it and to confront Jared when she got back home. She would go straight to him. But she would talk to Anne first.

They sat on the porch like that until dinner time. Neither of them saying anything but both understanding the immense pain of their plights. Ella Jean had not been able to save her daughter and the pain of discovering who she really was proved devastating. Pam had pretended for over five years that the warning signs were not glaring, where Jared and René were concerned. She, like her sister, saw what she wanted to see. Perhaps it was from all those years having to pretend things were alright in order to survive. They'd both learned to look passed the truth to survive and maybe it was time to stop.

Ella Jean broke the silence. "Let's get something to eat."

They went into the little house and began preparing a supper of baked fish and a salad with vegetables from Ella Jean's garden. Pam poured lemonade into two glasses filled with crushed ice. Ella Jean sat the two plates atop the blue placemats and carefully laid down a fork and a napkin. At the center of the table were a bottle of pickled peppers, a container of toothpicks and a bottle of hot sauce. They ate in silence, did the dishes and retired to their separate spaces.

Lying in the little pink room, Pam thought about all of it. There was too much to process. It was all just too much. Michelle was dead. She was too young to be dead. Rachel told her that she and Trent were going to stop trying to have a baby and look into adopting next year. They seemed happy with that decision. Reagan was pregnant and everybody was happy about that. They all needed new life. Before she left, Anne had promised to look in on René while Pam was in Mississippi. The movers had come and the unpacking would have to begin without her. Rae could get started. René needed to have a healthy baby and then they would deal with Jared. They needed to get her away from him and in a place where she could be safe. Ella Jean hadn't gone that far but Pam's mind had. She thought about Jared, and the deceit of it all, if it was true. *If he could pretend he was not with Michelle in the car accident, what else was he capable of?*

Ella Jean saw a dead bird that night in her own backyard when she took the trash out. She wanted to scream. Birds were turning up dead all the time and all the time in her path. Now her baby was dead and in the ground. She pulled the blue quilt up close and tucked it beneath her chin. The windows were open and the room was hot but the quilt made her feel less alone in the empty bed.

As she looked up from the bed into sheer darkness, Ella Jean thanked God for allowing her to survive. She thanked him for allowing her to survive the hell that was life with her mother, her pregnancy with Michelle and the cruelty and humiliation she endured with Michael Montgomery. She had survived and was still here. Daddy Sloane promised her that that which didn't kill her would make her stronger. She *was* stronger and growing stronger every day. Pam's presence in her home made the little house come alive. She wasn't so lonely and had enjoyed these days off from work. Reverend Franklin told her to take as much time as she needed and she was glad she'd taken his advice. Dead birds or no dead birds, she was going to make it.

In this world you will have tribulation, but be of good cheer, I have overcome the world.

Chapter 42

....

Ella Jean knew the day would be different just by the way it started. Reverend Franklin had been calling to check on her ever since Michelle died. She liked their talks and had grown accustomed to the nightly phone calls. It was a pleasant change because they never talked on the phone before Michelle passed away. They spoke every day at work, so there was really no need for much else. He didn't call last night but instead called bright and early this morning in the most wonderful mood. She was used to her weekly calls from Pam and the occasional call from some of the deaconesses at church, but other than that, her phone didn't ring. So she was startled when she hung up the phone after talking with the Reverend only to have it ring again. It wasn't even nine o'clock yet.

"Hello, may I speak with Ella Jean Washington?"

The voice on the phone sounded frail and unfamiliar.

"This is her speaking"

"Ella Jean, you don't remember me but I have been waiting a long time to see you again. I have something to give you and I need you to come and get it. It is yours."

"Who is this?" Ella Jean didn't want to be rude but she was feeling uneasy and she couldn't make out the voice on the other end of the phone.

"This is Mary. I'm so sorry that the child we worked so hard to get in the world is gone away from it. Please come today, my time here ain't long either."

The woman gave Ella Jean an address and directions that Ella Jean carefully wrote down on the pad next to the phone in the kitchen. After they both hung up, Ella Jean just sat there at the kitchen table as if she'd seen a ghost. Pam had been listening, drinking coffee across from her big sister.

"Who was that Ella Jean? Is everything alright?"

She wasn't sure if she could handle any more bad news. Ella placed the pad down on the table gingerly like it was a prized possession and got up to go to the sink. In route she turned to her sister.

"I need to ride off a piece this mornin'. You wanta come wit me?" Ella Jean began to wash her delicate coffee cup and saucer with the pale blue flowers on them. She placed them in her drying rack, thinking about the last time she heard Miss Mary's voice. She steadied herself on the sink and counter. This was a trip she had to take.

Pam didn't know how to answer or what to think. She'd never seen Ella Jean like this but knew she'd go with her.

"Ella Jean, how long will we be away and where are we going?"

"I'm leaving in an hour, Pam and it's something I have to do, something I just have to do. I don't have answers for your questions. I don't even have answers for mine, but I don't want to do this and having you with me will make it easier." Ella spoke honestly from her heart.

"I'll be ready," was Pam's only response.

The sisters drove for hours heading from Pascagoula to Tupelo, Mississippi. The GPS on Pam's phone said they could estimate arriving in five hours and fifteen minutes. Ella Jean said they'd be there in four hours if the traffic allowed. Pam texted Randolph and Anne to tell them both that she was heading to unknown territory. She wasn't sure what to expect, but she knew this was important. Before they left, Ella Jean told her to pack at least one change of clothes and something to sleep in. She did just as she was told and it transported her to their childhood. Before Ella Jean got pregnant with Michelle, she had been like Pam's mother. She always gave her clear directives, made sure her needs were met and that she was safe.

After they'd driven for three hours, Pam broke the silence. "Ella Jean, where are we going?"

"Pam, there was a lady at Missy's funeral sitting in the back on the last pew. She was old, I mean really old. Did you see her when we went out de church?"

"No Ella Jean. There were a lot people in the church that day. I don't remember any old lady. I'm sorry I didn't notice her. Is she one of Daddy Sloane's aunts?"

Ella paused and chose her words carefully. She had never spoken of any of this to a living soul.

"She is the woman who helped me to bring Missy into this world after her father left me with her with instructions to get rid of the baby and me too if there was any trouble."

"Oh, Ella Jean! No. Then why are we going back there? This is no good for you, for anybody. It's the past. It's done. Let's go back to Pascagoula." Pam was angry that Michelle's father had thought so little of her sister and she didn't want to hear any more. She wasn't sure she could handle the details.

Ella Jean kept her eyes on the road. She explained that they had to go. She said she needed to face the place and the memories she'd run from for so long. They continued north on Interstate 45 as if this was a planned road trip and nothing was wrong.

The two women pulled off the highway exit and went through the small town towards the outskirts. They headed down a dusty dirt road. It was almost three o'clock and a canopy of dark heavy clouds formed overhead with the promise of rain. The road wound itself through trees and overgrown brush. As they went farther fewer clapboard houses sat off in the distance. They pulled up to a dead end where a gray worn out house sat waiting for them. Ella Jean stopped the car, reclined back into the headrest with her eyes closed and began to moan softly. It was as if she was communing with things Pam was not privy to. Pam grabbed her sister's fleshy arm.

"Ella Jean, whatever it is. I'm here. We will face this together. It's the past. It's over. But if you don't want to go in it's not too late. We can turn this car around and high tale our butts right back where we came from." Pam tried to add levity to the situation and it might have worked.

"Girl, we are getting out of this car and going into that house. We come too far to turn back now, in more ways than one," Ella Jean chuckled through her fear and pain.

Before they reached the rickety porch, the door opened and a small woman stood smiling with two teeth missing in her mouth, one on the top and one on the bottom. She wore a red scarf on her small head with wisps of gray hair peeking through. Hanging off her thin frame was a faded cotton dress under a dingy apron with a torn pocket on which hung a string of safety pins. She looked like a witch from a horror film except for one thing. Her eyes were the warmest, deepest, golden brown eyes Pam had ever seen. They looked too young and misplaced against her deep sienna wrinkled skin.

"Y'all come in. I've been expectin' you." She reached for Ella Jean first and gave her a big hug, digging her boney fingers into Ella Jean's reluctant flesh. To Pam's surprise, Ella Jean returned the embrace and smiled. Then Miss Mary released Ella Jean and turned her attention to Pam.

"You must be Pam." She reached for Pam and hugged her so tightly that Pam could feel her tiny rib cage and soft flat breasts against her body.

"Yes, I'm Ella Jean's sister," she squeaked.

"I know. I know all about you and Daddy Sloane and that mama of yourn. Come in, I'm Miss Mary. Your sister and I became friends at a time in her life she really needed a friend. I been keeping up with her ever since."

They moved into the little house and Pam was surprised at how neat and clean the shot gun shack was. She could make out two rooms and a kitchen in the back. The three of them sat on a brown couch in the front room that was Miss Mary's living room. Miss Mary and Pam flanked Ella Jean as Pam waited to see what this strange visit was all about.

"I'm sorry about your baby Ella Jean." Miss Mary spoke, patting Ella Jean's hand.

Ella Jean didn't respond and Pam didn't know what would be the right response so she kept her mouth shut tight, staring at the woman who was staring at her sister. Miss Mary got up and went into the next room. Pam heard a drawer open and close and then the tiny octogenarian returned to the room like a little elf, carrying a manila envelope.

"I know you want to know why I asked you to come here Ella Jean." She placed the envelope in Ella Jean's lap.

"Open it."

Ella Jean looked at Pam and slowly opened the envelope. It had legal papers and a check. The numbers on the check were more numbers than Ella Jean had ever seen together before. $900,000. The check was made out to Ella Jean Washington. Ella showed the check to Pam as she questioned Miss Mary.

"What's this for? Who's it from? Who givin' me this kind of money?" She fired one question after another at Miss Mary.

"It's your money Ella Jean. It's all yours." Miss Mary smiled and nodded her head up and down.

Pam took the papers from the envelope and began to read through the legal documents. The money was from the estate of Dr. Michael Montgomery III. He died just four months ago having inherited the estates of his father and grandfather many years earlier. Dr. Montgomery was a very wealthy man in his seventies. It turns out he was stabbed to death by a twenty year old young woman he hired to clean his house. The woman confessed but claimed self-defense and was awaiting trial.

The family attorney called Mary to try and find Michelle as requested by Michael Montgomery II, Michelle's grandfather. The last will and testament left everything to Michelle or her surviving relatives upon his son's death. Michelle's father and Ella Jean's tormentor, Michael, had no idea that in his death, Ella Jean would get everything. He had long since forgotten her, he thought the baby was dead and Ella Jean, the casualty of a botched abortion. The family lawyers had done their part in keeping the secret they were paid well by his father to guard.

Ella Jean was inheriting two houses, both the grand family home in Tupelo and a vacation home in Biloxi. The will read that everything in the Montgomery family should go to Michael and in the event of his death they should go to his only daughter, Michelle. In the case that Michelle was no longer alive then the entire inheritance would go to her children unless there were none. In that case everything belonged to her mother –Ella Jean Washington.

Chapter 43

….

Ella Jean and Pam spent the rest of the evening asking questions and getting answers. Miss Mary prepared a dinner of fresh grouper, collard greens and corn bread and a mouthwatering peach cobbler for dessert. The time spent around her kitchen table revealed many secrets and Pam felt her sister was the bravest woman in the world to have survived the ordeal the two women described.

Miss Mary revealed that Ella Jean was the tenth young woman Michael Montgomery had dropped off for her to perform an illegal abortion on. She shared that many years before the girls started coming and both she and Michael were young, she was once in love with him and gave birth to his son. Michael refused to marry her and she refused to "take care of it." The little boy died mysteriously shortly before his fifth birthday and Mary was left alone, disgraced, distraught and penniless.

After her son's death she came to Mississippi to be close to Michael and to live with her aunt who was a midwife and helped women in trouble. There were many kinds of trouble a woman needed help with in those days and Mary was around to see it all. She taught Mary everything she knew and died leaving her the house and her job. Michael paid her every month until the day he died but Michelle was the last girl he sent to Mary to "help out."

Usually Mary made a tea for the girls to drink daily for about five days. The tea was made up of chamomile, parsley root, cohosh and tansy. It would be laced with a few ounces of turpentine and taken until the young women convulsed and bled. Most of them were sterile when they were sent back to Dr. Montgomery for his continued enjoyment. When he grew tired of using their young bodies, he would simply tell them, "My house no longer needs cleaning. It is clean enough." He'd then pay them enough money to leave, always saying it was just the back pay they had earned for taking such good care of his home and being so discrete. Grateful to get away and broken by the shame, they took the money and never said anything to anybody. He always got away with it. Until Ella Jean.

The night he'd dropped Ella Jean off she was already five months pregnant, too far along for any of Mary's teas or powders. Ella Jean fought for her life for one solid week while drifting in and out of consciousness. She wanted to keep her baby and made the mistake of telling Michael that. He beat her that night for one solid hour, blow after blow. She had to get away from Michael. Mary saw herself when she looked at the bruised shapely girl and made up her mind over the span of that week to help her in a different way. She patched her up and set the bones that were broken and nursed her back to health. Ella Jean spent one full month in the little house and grew stronger every day.

Mary told Dr. Montgomery that Ella Jean died. She had lost one other girl he sent to her so she knew what he would say. He instructed her to bury the body and sent a larger check that month. Mary didn't tell Ella Jean any of this, she simply put her on a bus headed home and prayed that she'd make it. Months went by and she kept praying that both Ella Jean and the baby would make it.

Months turned into years and she heard around town that Michael was still collecting and breaking girls for sport. He'd found another woman over in Meridian to do his "fixin" but the checks still came every month. Miss Mary explained to Pam and Ella Jean before they went to bed in her tiny house that night that she didn't want to be the only one who knew about the one Montgomery heir. Ella Jean was the only other girl besides Mary herself that wouldn't be forced into having an abortion. So she called Michael's father ten years after Ella Jean left her house and told him he had a grandchild in Pascagoula. She didn't know if it was a little girl or a little boy but she knew the mother's name and she knew they lived in Pascagoula.

Mary told Michael's father she would share the information on one condition, and that was that he would never tell his son. He promised and sent a private detective to get information on his heir. He was glad his wife was dead and didn't live to see what their son turned out to be. He sent Mary notes and newspaper clippings about Michelle's accomplishments and put money aside for her in a trust that his son knew nothing about. Miss Mary couldn't save her son and she couldn't save Ella Jean's daughter. Sitting in her little house, she was saddened that for all her trying, both of their babies were dead.

God is not mocked. Whatever a man sows he will reap.

Chapter 44

....

Reverend Franklin parked his car in Ella Jean's small gravel filled driveway. It was almost four o'clock on Friday and he wasn't used to being anywhere other than the parsonage or the church. If he wasn't at those two places, he was fishing with Frankie Bea. So everything about this seemed strange. But he had called Ella Jean and asked if he could come over and talk for a spell. She seemed surprised but had agreed he could call on her.

Pam had gone back to Annapolis after they returned from their two day trip that Ella Jean said she didn't want to talk about. Reverend Franklin put on his church suit and cologne. He never wore cologne, he hadn't since his wife died. He hadn't been with a woman in almost forty years and that was okay with him. He had the Lord, fishing, his son and his work. He also had Ella Jean's friendship. Working with her everyday was a joy to him and in so many ways she was like a wife to him. She had looked out for him and Frankie Bea for a long time.

Ella Jean heard the car engine turn off and peeked through the curtain. She didn't know why she was nervous. It was just Reverend Franklin and he'd been in her house many times. This was no different. It felt different though.

Everything was different. She missed her child. She was a rich woman now and Pam had told her not to tell anyone. She wanted to tithe, but Pam suggested she send an anonymous gift to the church and leave it between herself and God. Her rationale was that everybody and his mother was going to be coming out of the woodwork asking her for money. Pam was also worried that Ella Jean would be a target for burglary and all kinds of craziness if too many people knew about the money. So she had said nothing to anyone, not even Reverend Franklin.

The knock on the door startled her even though she watched the man walk up to it. Ella Jean smoothed out her gray and white floral dress and patted the top of her wig down. She put her hand in front of her mouth and blew out to check her breath. She felt stupid for doing that. This wasn't a date. She was almost sixty years old. Her only child turned out to be the worst kind of woman there is and was dead. There was nothing for her to be this happy about. She had money but so did Miss Mary, and she and many others were proof that money couldn't buy happiness. She opened the door.

"Good afternoon, Reverend. Come on in." Ella Jean smiled, nervously.

"Afternoon, Ella Jean, you look pretty."

Reverend Franklin had not planned to say that and was sorry the minute the words left his mouth. He didn't want to come on too strong and he didn't want to scare her away. Ella Jean did look pretty though.

He came into the living room. Moses Franklin was a big yellow man with freckles. His hair had tints of red and gray and looked like sheep's wool, thick and curly. His wife Bea had been a plump chocolate woman and if he had a type, then that's what it was: plump and chocolate. He smiled, unbuttoned his jacket and sat down on Ella Jean's couch.

Ella Jean offered him a choice of water, iced tea, lemonade or coffee. She didn't know why she said coffee. It was the middle of summer and hot outside. She was frustrated with herself for acting like this was a big deal and vowed to stop it immediately.

"I have some pound cake I made yesterday, would you like a slice, Reverend Franklin?" She asked as she walked into the kitchen to get the cake.

"I don't mind if I do. I'm not gonna sit up here and turn away pound cake, Miss Ella Jean," he chuckled.

Bringing the cake and the lemonade on a tray Pam had given her, she sat down next to her guest. The conversation started and seemed endless. They talked and they laughed. The television was on one of the religious channels but the volume was muted. It was eight o'clock and five hours had passed. They hadn't even eaten dinner. The large man rose from the couch.

"Well, Miss Ella Jean, I been at your house long enough. I'm going to go and let you get ready for bed." The thought of that aroused his curiosity and his body. He headed towards the door because he knew it was time to go. Ella Jean got up and followed behind Reverend Franklin and thanked him for coming to visit.

"It was a nice visit. Thanks for checking on me, Reverend Franklin."

"Call me Moses, Miss Ella Jean. You can call me Moses, God won't mind." He smiled and closed the door.

Ella Jean took a bath and went to bed without dinner. Reverend Moses Franklin called Ella Jean that night when he got home and asked if he could come to visit the next day after church or if she wanted to go to dinner after church. She agreed he could come over, and that is how it began. Moses Franklin saw Ella Jean Washington every night like clockwork, rain or shine. On Wednesday night he picked her up for bible study and waited until all the parishioners left and drove her home and sat in her living room. On Thursday night he followed her in his car home from choir rehearsal and they sat on her porch in the gliders. He stopped wearing his suit each visit and wore dress pants and a short sleeve shirt. They were courting and Ella Jean was happier than she had ever been.

One Sunday after church, he came over for dinner as was their new custom. Ella Jean made meatloaf and mashed potatoes with biscuits and green beans. They enjoyed her homemade sweet potato pie for dessert. Ella Jean liked using her dining room on Sundays. The couple sat at the long cherry wood table and talked about his sermon and the nice couple from Mobile that joined church. Moses Franklin cleared his throat and his hands started to sweat. He had prayed about what he was about to say and asked God for guidance. Excusing himself from the table, he went into the living room where his jacket was draped on the back of Ella's couch. The little box in his jacket pocket felt tiny in his massive hands and the walk back into the dining room seemed a mile long.

He sat down and Ella Jean wondered if he'd had to go to the bathroom. Placing the box on the table, the God-fearing man began the words he'd rehearsed for weeks as he stood in front of her.

"Ella Jean, by now, you know how I feel about you. I love you and I have for some time. I'm sorry Michelle is gone. I hate anything that hurts you. But I believe that God has a plan and that good can come even from sorrow. If you want to live in my house we can do that. If you want to live here we can do that. If you want me to buy you a new house and start over from scratch we can do that. We can get brand new furniture too. I got some money saved up and I ain't as poor as I look. "

Ella Jean started to feel faint. This was not supposed to be happening. What was he doing? The nervous man continued with his speech.

"If I try and get down on my knees I might not get up so I'm just gonna bow a little bit and go on and ask you. Will you do me the honor of being my wife?"

Ella Jean said one word amidst many tears. "Yes."

Weeping may endure for a night but joy comes in the morning.

Chapter 45

….

The call from Ella Jean early that morning brought Pam pure joy. Her sister was getting married! It was funny how things worked. After the trip back from Tupelo, Pam had not had time to process all that she now knew. But everything made more sense. Michelle's death and that god-awful diary were such negative things but they had brought about some very positive things. She and Ella Jean talked on the phone every day since Michelle died. They were closer and she knew Reverend Franklin was going to ask her to marry him because he had hinted around to that end the last time she saw him.

Jared had moved out of the townhouse after Pam and Anne talked with René. They made her promise that she would minimize her contact with him. Nobody knew where he was. Jackson confirmed that he had requested use of his accrued sick leave and was not reporting to work. René was staying with her sister, Rachel in D.C. for a while because at this point in her pregnancy, she really needed to take it easy. Pam had not told Randolph about Jared's affair with Michelle but just the idea of it made her sick to her stomach. René was safe and that was all that mattered now. She just wouldn't allow herself to think about Jared, and Michelle was dead.

She and Ella Jean had slept like babies at Mary's house and driven back home, feeling as if burdens had been lifted.

Ella Jean hadn't seen a dead bird since they returned and since she, Anne, Rachel and Reagan had packed things up for René and driven with her to Rachel and Trent's place, the dreams had vanished. She hadn't had one in a while. Things were looking up in spite of the craziness.

Pam and Randolph would move to Virginia Beach in just a few days. Rae was already back at school and had done the walk-through for their home in Virginia Beach for them while Pam was visiting Ella Jean. All but the master bedroom, Randolph's office, and a skeleton of kitchen items were boxed up and ready to go. They had a couple of loose ends to tie up, and then they would be on their way. Anne and Jackson were scheduling their move to the west coast in two months. Pam would miss them and the Naval Academy but was used to the constant change. She wanted René to come with her and have the baby in Virginia Beach, but René wanted Doctor Walker to deliver her baby because that was who she trusted. Pam was not going to give up without a fight.

René had decided to file for a divorce. There was no possibility of reconciliation at this point. She said the thought of Jared made her sick and Pam cautioned all of the girls to limit the conversation about him and the affair. Her daughter was pregnant and she didn't need any more pain or drama.

Everyone was excited about Reagan's pregnancy. Sean was beaming and Reagan had already decided that if it was a girl they were going to name the baby, Grace. She said God had been forgiving and merciful and shown her unmerited favor and that is what grace was. Unmerited favor. When asked what the plan for a boy's name was, she shrugged,

"He might just be Grace too! Deal with it." She laughed so hard at that.

"Girl, you are not going to name your son Grace," Anne chimed in.

They packed René's suitcases to head out of the home she was no longer willing to share with Jared. The room erupted in laughter. In true Reagan style, the situation was infused with a bit of mirth. Pam was sure that things were going to be okay. She just had to make sure Jared did not attend the Change of Command. She didn't want René to have to see him and as René's mother, she couldn't be sure what she'd do or say if she saw him.

René told them everything. She'd shared everything except the fact that Jared hit her. She knew if her family knew and if Jackson and Anne knew and if Trent and Sean knew, it would be like throwing kerosene on a raging fire. She decided she would never see Jared again. She couldn't find it in her heart to forgive him and she wondered what kind of wife that made her and what kind of Christian it made her. René wondered if she'd ever really loved her husband. She was certain she had but no man was going to hit her. She was uneasy about not hearing from him or knowing his whereabouts. She didn't feel safe.

Even though I walk through the valley of death, I will fear no evil, because you are with me.

Chapter 46

....

Jared dialed his wife's number for the fifteenth time. She obviously had his number blocked. The call went straight to voicemail. He punched the wall and regretted it as blood trickled from his knuckles. He wondered how this happened. Things went too wrong too fast. One minute he was married to the girl of his dreams, amassing a fortune and about to be a father, and the next minute he is sneaking in a hospital room with an anti-diabetic drug he'd gotten from Tony's samples. It was a drug called rosiglitazone and he'd done his research. He'd dropped by that night to talk about Michelle and see how she was doing. Tony thought it was because he was a concerned husband. He'd stolen several pharmaceutical samples he thought he could use and worst case scenario, he'd use them all. He'd gone through the bag when Tony left the room to get them beers. He was looking for something to make it look like a heart attack and he hit the jackpot. The right amount of rosiglitazone would throw the patient into cardiac arrest and that's exactly what happened when he injected it into the top of Michelle's IV drip bag. The hole left by the needle was microscopic and the air it let in was as dangerous as the drug itself. Her official cause of death was cardiac arrest and no one questioned it, because of her condition. Jared decided nobody knew and nobody would know. Michelle was buried and so was the affair.

Jared stood in the hotel room with his bloody hand wrapped in a towel as he fixed his eyes and energy on the dented wall and waited for his phone to ring. He was going to the Change of Command Ceremony, all right, and nobody was going to stop him. He'd see his wife and end this whole thing once and for all. Jared had already made a call about taking care of things and once he got the details ironed out, made the payment and made sure his plane was waiting, things would be all set. He'd take his wife and son out of the country without a trace. He'd be in a military plane and in uniform, if he could just stay ahead of Randolph, Jackson and the Navy Inspector General.

The phone rang and the voice on the other end sounded eager to take the job. The guy knew his last name and said he'd heard a lot about him from their mutual contact. Jared didn't care. He hung up the phone, but before he did, he repeated his instructions so there would be no mistaking what the man was getting $10,000 for.

"Just make sure Randolph Hamilton is dead."

...And you will know the truth and the truth will set you free.

Chapter 47

….

Randolph and his friend Jackson sat behind the Commandant and the Deputy Commandant as they listened to Senator John McCarr address the body of midshipmen. There was a sea of navy blue uniforms and they all sat listening attentively. Jackson's wife Anne sat next to him. Generally, they attended these things as a foursome and went to dinner afterwards, but not this night. On this occasion, Pam said she had a headache and didn't feel up to it.

The Superintendent of the Naval Academy stood at the podium to thank one of their most famous alumni for coming to speak and to present a perfunctory plaque. The speech had been average, but the midshipmen were an attentive audience. They filed out of the David Robinson Alumni Hall after shaking hands with their speaker and exchanging pleasantries.

Jackson had come across some emails that presented a bit of a security breach right before Michelle died, and the issue dominated his thoughts. He kind of wanted to run it by Randolph because that's what he would normally do. But this time was different. His staff assistant had done some preliminary research last week. By all indications the active duty individual that appeared to be involved was Jared Foster Reed. This made it complicated. Jackson didn't want to compromise the investigation but he also wanted his friend's opinion and perhaps more importantly, he wanted to alert him. If René was in danger and something happened to her, he'd never forgive himself. The three friends walked back across the yard, passing the stoic Naval Academy Chapel and headed towards Porter Road.

Anne played with the red and gold beads on her three Pandora charm bracelets. Her red wool sweater dress contrasted with the two deep blue uniforms decorated with their gold buttons and ribbons. She was glad she wore the black low heeled pumps tonight instead of the heeled boots she'd intended to wear. They allowed her to comfortably keep up with the swift steps of her escorts. Her thoughts were on the member of their foursome who wasn't there. She was worried about Pam. The two men, almost as if in formation, walked on either side of her in silence. Anne knew that Jackson had uncovered information that pointed to Jared being involved in some nasty stuff. She also knew that Pam didn't trust Jared. She'd promised Jackson she wouldn't say anything to Pam but she wasn't sure she could keep that promise.

Jackson talked to Anne about it a couple of months ago and she had urged him to speak with Randolph right away. The three of them arrived at Jackson and Anne's quarters first and Anne kissed Randolph on the cheek, making her exit so the two friends could talk. Walking swiftly up the stairs she teased,

"Tell that wife of yours she owes me big time…leaving me to suffer through that boring lecture and listening to the two of you talk shop all evening. She owes me and I'm going to collect."

Randolph smiled and nodded his affirmation.

"Will do, ma'am."

He gave her a little salute as she closed her front door, leaving the two of them in front of the house in the dark coldness of night. Anne went to the kitchen and picked up the wall phone receiver. She thought about calling Pam, but was afraid she'd say too much so she put it down and poured a glass of scotch, plunked two ice cubes in it and waited for Jackson to come inside.

Standing in the front of his assigned quarters, Jackson thought about how working so closely with his best friend's son-in-law had come about. He requested Jared to be on his staff as a favor to Randolph, who felt he could benefit from the mentoring Jackson's leadership would provide. Jackson liked Jared well enough and was pleased with his job performance overall until now. He didn't see this coming and he wasn't sure how it could be possible.

"So what'd you think about the lecture? The facts McCarr presented were very relevant and the plebes needed to know that stuff. It was good."

As Randolph began reflecting on the lecture that consumed the last hour they'd spent together, Jackson worried about how to begin the conversation he knew they must have. They had been through a lot together and their names were on the "Flag List." They were both about to obtain the rank of admiral (07). There was so much to celebrate. Jackson would be headed to Mayport and Randolph to Norfolk in just a few weeks, and then this.

"Randolph, some interesting data has been presented to me from Intel," Jackson eased into the topic.

"Yeah really, what's going on?" Randolph listened without much interest.

"The Wiki leak situation has taken an unusual turn and implicated something that could prove devastating for our national security. It would impact you, Pam and the girls and it's serious. It's bad Randolph." Jackson looked around and stared his friend in the eye and spoke just above a whisper.

"What are you talking about, Jack?" Randolph felt uncomfortable but remained calm. He always remained calm. In fact, he wore calm.

"Intel claims to have proof that Jared is involved in selling military secrets to Russian operatives. It appears he's been doing it for a few years and that he provided information linked to the Ukrainian situation and the ground breaking Russian, Chinese alliance. Apparently Jared has been under investigation for about a year. "

Randolph thought about his daughter, René. She was pregnant with this man's baby. He thought about Pam and how tired and frail she seemed lately. Finally, he thought about the delicate state of the SOCOM and CENTCOM missions Jared was involved in. He thought of himself and his reputation and his culpability in this. He tightened his jaw.

"Let's talk tomorrow, off the yard. I need to know everything you know."

Jackson nodded and turned to climb the stairs and go inside to Anne. He knew she'd be waiting with a scotch and soda for both of them and tonight he needed it. He didn't look back as Randolph continued down Porter Road to his quarters. Jackson had wrestled with this thing for several months now and they would finally talk. To both men this felt catastrophic.

Chapter 48

....

Randolph walked up the two flights of stairs that wound their way to the master bedroom. The house was dark and old but Pam had made it feel like home. Even though most of their household goods were boxed up, she still cooked dinner and things still ran smoothly. He didn't know how she did it but he was grateful that she did. Wherever they lived, wherever the Navy sent them, their home was warm and welcoming and tonight it smelled like something sweet. Randolph decided it smelled like coconut. He'd eaten his dinner of blackened fish and roasted vegetables quietly with Pam before the lecture and there was no trace of fish odor in the house. Pam had barely said a word during dinner and that wasn't like her. She was always engaging. They talked about everything, they always had. She was hiding something, but then so was Randolph.

As he opened the door, she sat up in the bed in white long sleeve silk pajamas with two pin curls in the front of her hair and gave him a weak smile. Something was wrong. She looked even more stressed than she had before he left for the Forestall Lecture. He decided not to talk to her about this mess with Jared until he could sort it out, until he got more details.

"How was Senator McCarr's talk, anything new?" Pam questioned just to be polite.

"It was fine, just more of the same. It was well received." He could tell by her tone that she wasn't really interested.

He began to take the medals and ribbons off his uniform and place them neatly in the velvet lined wooden box on his dresser. Hanging the uniform neatly on his side of the closet amid the rows of navy blue, white and khaki uniforms, he grabbed a clean t-shirt and drawstring cotton pajama pants and headed to the bathroom to shower.

The handsome middle aged man graying at the temples climbed under the sage green cotton duvet next to his wife and moved all the unnecessary pillows off the bed, tossing them gently onto the chair closest to his side.

"So that's what we do now, Randolph? We play basketball with *my* silk pillows?" Pam spoke in mock anger as she rose up on her elbow frowning at her husband.

Randolph chuckled, "Nothing hit the floor. They landed neatly on the chair. You know you married a well-coordinated part-time athlete and full-time warrior."

Pam giggled, "Right. I forget both the athletic and the warrior part, *old* warrior. Sometimes I forget."

Pam snuggled up next to this man who could still make her laugh no matter what was going on in the world and rested her head on his chest. She thought about how her sister's life had changed the three months since Michelle's death. Randolph welcomed her with an outstretched arm that folded gently across her soft brown breasts. The silk pajama top felt good on his bare skin. She fit neatly in his arms and they said nothing for a while.

She had spent a week with her sister after her niece died and she was glad to be back at home. Randolph was happy about the news of Ella Jean's wedding and so were the girls. They were planning to get married at Christmas time. Randolph and the kids couldn't believe that Ella had inherited so much money. She hadn't told Reverend Franklin about it at first, so they all knew he was marrying her because he loved her. But after all these years, nobody doubted that anyway. Pam didn't tell Randolph about Michelle's diary or the affair. She knew she had to tell him something though, so she spoke up,

"Randolph, René is going to spend a few days with Rachel in the city because she needs to be looked after. I'm getting ready for the move and she doesn't want to come to Virginia and let me look after her. With all the boxes and commotion I can hardly blame her. Rachel's working from home and so we've decided that'd be the best place for her now. You and I both know, she shouldn't even be pregnant."

Randolph rubbed his wife's silk clad arm.

"What does Jared think about all of this? Why can't he look after his wife? "

Pulling the propped up pillows down to lay flat on the bed she positioned herself on her side facing her husband and decided to say nothing more about it. She prayed for René before drifting off to sleep. Randolph pulled her close to him and reassured her with his words and his touch despite his own suspicions and his earlier conversation with Jackson.

"Get some sleep. It'll be okay; don't let yourself get worked up just yet. Let's find out what's really going on."

Pam lifted the covers up around her face and drifted off to sleep feeling proud that she'd emptied her pill bottles down the toilet. It was one of the hardest things she'd ever done. Anne had made her promise to see someone and stop and each day it got a little better. She hadn't had a headache since she'd been back and hoped and prayed the worst of it was behind her.

Randolph waited until she was asleep and slipped out of their bed. Grabbing his navy blue wool USNA robe he quietly climbed the staircase to his small third floor office and sat down at the desk. He adjusted his eyes to the light from the monitor and began to type lightly. There. He was in. His Common Access Card (CAC card) allowed him access to the restricted files, the Department of Defense network and computer systems from his home. He typed in his passwords and began reading the classified files Jackson had forwarded.

The list of classified briefings and plans was endless and they were building a case with his connection with the Russians and his involvement in the annexing of Crimea. In addition to that, it appears Jared's name was the common denominator in over a dozen failed missions. Each time there was a security breach, he was connected with the project or had access. It was damning. Jackson had cause for alarm. Randolph would meet with the I.G. and let them know he was available in any capacity necessary to take this creep down. He was a fraud and the lowest type of traitor. Jared had to be stopped.

Part IV

Winter

The Promise of Peace

Chapter 49

....

What is this? The black St. John knit skirt stretched across the roundness of her hips. An area filled with nickel size bumps and lumps glared back from the mirror in defiance. "Damn this cellulite." Pulling a mid-thigh length black Spanx from the top drawer of the Ethan Allen cherry wood lingerie chest, Pam sat down on the bed to remove all traces of an aging rear end from her slender frame. She had always been confident about the visual statement her body made. Forget Zumba and all of that. Moderation was the key. She preferred walking to the gym and believed eating right and getting rest was good enough.

There. She wrestled the black spandex shorts up her thighs and butt. Thank God for real underwear. What was this new generation of thong wearers going to do when the lumps appeared? *After sporting dental floss strings in their cracks for decades, how would they transition when the fat coagulated on their butts? Maybe they'd line up in greater groves to get it professionally sucked out. Yes, that's it. They'd get liposuction with the ease that her mother's generation had gotten press and curls every two weeks.*

She thought of her daughters, Rachel, Reagan, René, and Rae. Their jelly bean colored underwear was made from less than 1/16 of a yard of fabric. Rae was in her room getting dressed. Pam could not believe that this would be her senior year at Georgetown. She'd come home earlier in the week and had been slow to get moving this morning. As for the older girls, they'd better be on time. This day was an important day whether they knew it or not. Randolph had worked hard and it had to be about him today. Regardless of what was going on with Jared, this day was about their father, it was his Change of Command. Pam's thoughts were interrupted by the loud ringing of the phone.

"This is Pam."

"Why so formal, Mom? It's just me." Pam didn't admit that without her reading glasses, it was impossible to read the caller ID. Time changes everything.

"Good morning, Rachel. Where are you?"

"I'm ten minutes away, Mom, log off with the crispness. I hear the stress in your voice."

"I'm fine. Your father is expecting us and Admiral MulRenéy is with him. Be late and see what happens. We are not keeping the CNO waiting. You know the traffic will be heavy. We need to allot enough time to get to the base."

"Have you talked to Reagan? She's chronically late not me. That's who you need to be worrying about. Mom, I've got to take another call. It's Trent. I'll be there in ten minutes. René is safe at home, she was in bed when I left and everything is going to be fine. The doors are locked and you know our building has a concierge and doorman. It's like Fort Knox. Jared will not be able to get to her. So don't worry. We'll look good, we'll make dad look good and all will be right with the world. This is going to be everything you want it to be, I promise. Bye."

Lowering the sage green phone to its receiver after the abrupt click, Pam thought about how she and Randolph had bought this house with the plans to retire in it. They were getting close. This was more than likely going to be the last tour and then they'd just enjoy each other and stay put. Her thoughts turned to Reagan. Where was she? She picked up the phone's receiver and put it down again. She thought better of calling.

"*Give me some space*." Pam heard Reagan's voice in her head. She'd show up. She always did but she and Sean seem so happy now that they were going to be parents. Pam thought about the darn yellow fingernail polish Reagan wore to her cousin's funeral just a few months ago and whispered a silent prayer that being pregnant would tone her "high fashions" down a bit.

Sitting at her dressing table's vanity mirror, Pam admired her own honey colored- skin. Many shades darker than most of Randolph's black friends' wives, she found some strange sense of victory in not being "high yellow" or "light skinned." She was decidedly brown. She had nothing against her many fair skinned friends, they were beautiful too. She found beauty to be beyond color. But she liked the fact that Randolph didn't think a size four blonde or a near white black woman the perfect accruement of success. She was bigger and blacker, and it suited her fine.

Pam unwrapped and unpinned her hair thinking that Keisha had done a great job getting the gray out. She was glad to be back in Hampton Roads with her regular hairdresser. Keisha had done her hair off and on for twenty years. The salons in Annapolis never worked out and she ended up driving in to D.C. or Baltimore for a nice style. She admired the side parted sepia bob that combed out nicely to hang just below her diamond-studded ears. The Ruby Woo MAC lipstick made her full lips the center of attraction on her face. She placed the final touch of blue- black mascara on her lashes and pushed back the pink chintz-covered chair. Wearing black sheer pantyhose, her knit skirt and matching shell, her toes sank into the plush sage green carpet as she stepped into her expansive closet to select a jacket. Scanning the rows of conservative garments, she searched for a black St. John knit jacket. The clothes were organized by color and purpose. They went from dark to light and formal to casual. There were 20 black knit jackets in a neat row. She gently selected a V-neck long sleeved one without a collar. It was embellished with silver metal bars on the cuffs. The stretch knit suits were not particularly cute to her. She found most of the styles dry and boring. It wasn't that she loved them. They were just incredibly forgiving and a size eight fit sleek and smooth over a size ten body.

Although she missed living on the yard, she was happy that they were back in Virginia Beach and back in their house. The renters had been kind this time unlike the last time where they had to replace carpet and re-wall paper rooms where kids had written on the walls. Pam thought about the life she and Randolph had built. They had four grown daughters, good investments and were still in love. It was going to be alright. She was so far away from the turmoil of her childhood. Daddy Sloane promised it would be all right if you just had faith and put your trust in God. This is what he meant. She repeated to herself out loud.

"It will be alright."

Today they would attend Randolph's change of command. He had just recently been promoted to admiral and gotten his first star. Today he would become the leader of Commander Cruiser Destroyer Group Eight (COMCRUDESGROU8). This put him in position for the twilight tour, his last tour in the Navy. There was talk of him going on and possibly getting another star but that's not what Pam wanted. They'd given so much. They both loved their country. They were patriots. How could they not be? Their slave ancestors had built much of this country and African Americans had fought in every war. Their roots were in Africa but their blood was in America and they had bled and died, often fighting other Americans for their full place in this country.

Even though they believed fighting for their flawed democracy to be a noble calling, Randolph and Pam were growing tired and after thirty years was feeling ready to retire and enjoy life. He'd missed so much of his girls growing up and now with two grandchildren on the way, he'd told Pam that he didn't want to miss anything else. She felt like this position promised stability in the near future. Everybody would be at the ceremony. One big happy family would be the presentation, regardless of the reality, regardless of Jared and what she knew.   She began to faintly sing a song from church,

"Faithful, faithful, faithful is our God…"

Chapter 50

....

"Mom, are you up there?" The familiar voice yanked her out of her own head.

Rachel appeared in the doorway with her father's grin and Pam couldn't help but marvel. Perfect teeth, framed with simple pale pink gloss covered pink brown lips. What a beautiful woman, she thought. Rachel, with Pam's beautiful full and expressive almond shaped brown eyes, was stunning. It seemed that since she and Trent had decided on adoption, she had more peace and a glow about her. She looked beautiful, but even as a small girl, folks had teased that her thick eyelashes could be mistaken for false ones. Now, augmented with expensive mascara and taupe, gold and brown eye shadow, they were perfect. She sported a longer, blacker version of her mother's bob and a kelly green tailored Misook suit with a double strand of pink-tinged pearls.

Rachel interrupted her mother's fawning thoughts. She hated the way her mother doted on her and acted as if she could do no wrong. She thought she was far from perfect, she thought, *just ask Trent.*

"So mom where is everybody? I thought Reagan's late behind would be here by now. I'm 30 minutes late myself, "she teased.

Pam thought before speaking.

"You know how Reagan is. She has to stop for coffee or something to eat at the airport. As skinny as she is, she's continuously eating. She's always running into her students and stopping to talk to people she knows. She'll be here."

Rachel looked at her Michael Kors rose watch and hoped that her sisters would be on time. She'd felt over the last couple of months since Michelle's funeral that her mother was a bit fragile. She didn't want anything to give her one of her "headaches."

She looked at her mother sitting at her vanity.

"What mom? Why are you staring? The suits wrong, right? I started to wear a black one, but I knew you'd have on black and I didn't want to do the whole 'matchy' thing and be corny…"

"No, you look perfect. There's nothing wrong with you, nothing." Pam smiled warmly and sounded a little too enthusiastic.

"Well, of course there isn't. That's why you should have named her Polly!" Reagan, pushed passed her sister in the doorway and plopped herself on the pink floral damask overstuffed chair next to her parents' four-poster bed, throwing her huge gray Prada bag on the ottoman in front of it. Smiling at her older sister, she blurted,

"Polly Perfect!"

"Don't hate," Rachel squealed with an amused smile.

Hearing the voice of her older sisters, Rae emerged half dressed, laughing at Reagan's eclectic ensemble. Rachel took in the full view of her sister too, and they both waited with great patience for their mother's next words. This was the yellow nail polish at the funeral and everything else. This was The Reagan and Pam Show. They could predict their mother's word and recite them in their minds along with her…. predictable, like clockwork, the familiar dance would begin. 1. 2. 3.

"Reagan, what are you wearing? It's winter in Virginia and you are pregnant. Where is your coat?"

Pam began the fashion war with her predictable first volley. "What?" Reagan grinned, feigning surprise. "What's wrong with it?" She grew tired of her mother's need for visual uniformity.

"Gangstahs don't get cold," she teased.

Reagan was beautiful, but this was not the occasion for a cropped sweater and leggings.

Reagan and Pam began to battle over Reagan's wardrobe choices from the time she was three begging to wear sundresses in the dead of winter when they were stationed in Rhode Island. Pam loved that her daughter was a free spirit and a creative soul. She had nurtured this in each of them. It was her gift to them.

These senseless battles were a source of amusement to René, Rachel and Rae but an irritant for Randolph. He'd worn a uniform since he was a seventeen-year-old midshipman at the Naval Academy and had no tolerance for or understanding of nonconformity. Now his second progeny stood before her mother and sisters, tall and regal but dressed like Eartha Kitt's Cat Woman. Pam firmly declared, "this is not going to work." Before Pam could say anything else…

"This here be America, chile!"

The room burst with laughter as all eyes took in the young woman standing in the doorway.   The three sisters all looked shocked to see René. Suddenly the amusement of the familiar game that had played out so often in their childhood, "Reining in Reagan," was of no consequence. René was supposed to be in bed at Rachel's house in D.C.

René's designer scent met the three women before she did and the room broke into squeals, tight hugs and pure joy. Baby girl was in the house! René wasn't supposed to be there and they were silently agreeing to put that on hold for a moment and just enjoy that she could be a part of this time after all she had been through recently.

"Mama said you weren't coming"

Reagan looked at her younger sister in sheer disbelief.

"Well, mama don't run me. I love my daddy just like y'all do and I wouldn't miss this for the world. Lord knows Reagan needs an ally when ambushed by Mom and Rachel. That's where I come in."

 She glanced playfully at her tall sister and winked a tired but mischievous brown eye.

René teased, "this be a free country, let the girl express her extraordinary sense of new baby mama style."

She entered the doorway, with a presence that defied her petite form and hugged Reagan.

René playfully chided, "do you, boo."

Pam was not amused. "So what else did you pack, Reagan?"

Reagan kissed her mother on the cheek, rubbing her tense shoulders. "Relax mom, I brought something that will suit your rigid requirements."

Chapter 51

....

Pam's eyes examined her pregnant daughter from head to toe, taking it all in. She tried to ignore the truth she knew. She hadn't seen her in three weeks but she'd talked to her every day. Seeing René now, Pam saw fatigue, despite her best attempts to look rejuvenated and the picture of pregnant health. She wore the perfect navy blue maternity pant suit with matching low heeled boots and navy kid gloves. Her bright paisley silk scarf was not enough to hide the fatigue lines.

Her hair hung in black soft girls around her shoulders. She'd given up relaxing her hair with chemicals after marrying Jared. Pam never understood why it took marrying a white man to liberate the kinks in her hair. But now she had the most beautiful natural ringlets that came from something she called thermal treatments that was really an updated pressing comb. Pam winced as she took in the dark circles under her daughter's eyes and a sadness that betrayed her smile as she and her sisters huddled. They patted her belly and talked about the baby. It was good to have them all together. These were the moments Pam lived for. She was excited about the baby and determined to do whatever it took to make sure René was going to be okay. They would be fine.

René thought about Jared and her doctor's orders. She knew she was putting herself and the baby at risk taking the quick flight from D.C. to Norfolk. She'd booked her flight a soon as she agreed to move in with Rachel and Trent. There was no way she was going to miss her father's Change of Command Ceremony. She had married Jared and they were getting a divorce if it was the last thing she did. It was not about his race. This was about a cheating husband. She would not let her messed up marriage or her frail health keep her from supporting her father.

René was glad she came and would make a point not to be alone with her mother at any time during the ceremony. She didn't want a lecture and she had no desire to talk about her failed marriage. Jared had better not show up and she hoped to God, Tony Green would stay away too.

The mood was tense and every member of the family had their own issues to confront.

Rae had talked to Frankie Bea at Michelle's funeral and he was convinced that Michelle was murdered. Even she thought that was a little over the top. She, who saw a mystery or a conspiracy behind every door, wasn't sure she believed anyone would want to kill Michelle. What would the motive have been? Instead, she thought that Frankie Bea just loved Michelle and couldn't bear to believe she was gone. He'd told Rae that he was not going to rest until he saw Michelle's murderer behind bars or dead.

Pam knew it was time to leave for the ceremony. Ella Jean, Reverend Franklin, Randolph's brother and his wife along with his parents were planning to meet them at the

Naval Station. They'd come in last night and were staying at the Navy Lodge. Although Pam was honestly excited about seeing her sister with her new fiancé, she was feeling overwhelmed and needed something to help her get through the day. She wasn't in any real physical pain but she needed a pill, just to take the edge off of her anxiety.

> *"Dear Lord, give me the strength to get through this day without a pill. I surrender this pain to you and ask that you help me to be a true help mate to Randolph and represent you in all I say and do today. Help me to see Jared as you see him. Take the hate from my heart. In Jesus' name, Amen."*

Chapter 52

....

"Okay, let's get in the car." Pam examined herself for the last time walking atop the soft beige carpet of the family room. She called to the girls and they suddenly emerged from the kitchen with muffled laughs. Regan had changed into a simple gray shift dress. It was long sleeved, without a collar and topped just above her gray stocking glad knees. Around her neck was draped a gray, black and navy scarf, adorned with geometric shapes. Today, she wore sensible Jimmy Choo gray suede pumps. Her neat braids cascaded over her broad shoulders and she looked wonderful.

"I'm glad you changed. You look smart," Pam rubbed Reagan's back as she inspected each of her daughters.

Reagan smiled thinking about how her mom always strived for visual perfection. When she was younger it pissed her off. She felt bound and trapped by the scrutiny. Now she simply understood it as her mother's need for order. It was her way of making sense of the world. Dad was in and out and the houses and cities always changed. She could control how things looked even if she couldn't control where she was. She equated her aesthetic with order and calm. Reagan thought of how Pam used to admonish, "you can't see the flowers in a vase if there is a sock on the floor."

Their homes were always well decorated and clean. Pam was meticulous about things matching and looking nice. Presentation was everything. Reagan and Rachel thought this was normal for the longest time. They thought everybody

had a housekeeper until that day at Keller High School when a girl had called them uppity black heifers for having her grandmother's best friends' as their maid. Their world was different from many of their school friends but by the time they figured that out it was too late to change.

"Am I driving?"

Rachel searched her mother's purse for car keys and looked around at the group of women.

René playfully snatched the keys from her hand.

"Let mom drive, ain't nobody tryin' to die today!"

Pam extended her open palm for the keys as she turned off the lights and set the alarm on the smooth ecru wall. Rachel, known for her road rage, gave them up reluctantly but without protest. She wanted today to go smoothly for her mom. That was the objective. They took the elevator down to the four car garage of their Georgian style home. Randolph added the elevator when his knees started to go bad four years ago. The girls piled in with Pam, Rachel and Rae taking the lead. René and Reagan were the last to board. All thoughts were on René. The elevator doors opened and they filed out of the stainless steel door.

As she drove from Virginia Beach into Norfolk, Pam's thoughts drifted to the many military moves. They'd moved fifteen times in their marriage of three decades. She thought of their first duty station in San Diego and the beautiful home they bought near the beach. It was a salmon colored stucco house with a garden of birds of paradise, citrus trees and one avocado tree. Living there before the girls were born had been fun. The wardroom parties she volunteered to host as a junior officer's wife, were legendary. She watched the top brass and decided then that she wanted that for Randolph. He deserved it. The next move was to Newport, Rhode Island for Naval War College. Pam was six months pregnant with René when they moved there, going from sunny citrus filled California to a place so cold that their first Easter egg hunt was held on a blanket of snow. It was jolting.

Each move meant new schools and new churches, libraries, grocery stores and finding new safe and familiar places. It often meant a revolving door of friends. Friends you leave and new friends to make and always perfecting goodbye. The moves took place in the summers and if you had an August birthday that was a guarantee of no friends at your birthday party because you didn't have time to make any. The girls became friendly and outgoing really fast. The costs were great too but there were so many benefits. Randolph had promised her over thirty-five years ago, they'd live happily ever after and this was the beginning of the fulfillment of his promise.

"Mom, are you okay?" Rachel had apparently been calling her for several minutes.

"Yes, I'm fine. I'm excited for your dad and glad that he is closer to his goals," Pam lied, keeping her eyes fixed to the road ahead.

Chapter 53

….

Anne leaned forward, flipped the vanity mirror on the passenger side of the car down and carefully applied orange-red lipstick. She reached into her navy blue Coach bag and found a tissue and placed it between her lips, opening and closing her mouth in quick little motions allowing them to press against the tissue. Jackson took his eyes off the road and glanced at his wife. Her blonde shoulder length hair was thick and fell softly around her face. The turned up ends lay comfortably on her red suit jacket. She wasn't wearing a blouse, just a strand of pearls and her small freckled breasts peeped out from the jacket closure. The red skirt rested on her knees and she wore sensible navy blue pumps. Jackson still found her alluring after thirty-five years together.

"Why do you put it on if you are only going to take it off with tissue? The lipstick, I mean," he questioned.

Anne chuckled.

"I'm not really taking it off. I'm making it less harlot-like."

"Oh, I see." Jackson smiled. "Well we certainly wouldn't want you to arrive at Randolph's Change of Command Ceremony looking like a harlot."

They drove in silence for the next thirty minutes while the voices of NPR went on about unrest in the Middle East and such. Jackson turned off the radio.

"Is Pam okay, Anne?" He asked with a look of intense pain in his eyes.

"I don't know. I know she's worried about René and she's tired," was all Anne could think to say.

"You know, Anne, this thing with Jared is pretty conclusive. It's coming to a head and they're closing in on him. I think they are going to make an arrest soon." Jackson looked straight ahead at the stretch of Interstate 50 leading to the Beltway.

"How can they do that when no one knows where he is?" Anne was worried.

"They are betting that he will come to the ceremony today. He's not the kind of guy who will stay away. My bet is he'll show up in arrogance and defiance. When he does Anne…" Jackson hesitated, knowing he shouldn't reveal all that he knew.

"When he does what, Jackson?" Anne was scared.

"Don't worry about it. They want him at that ceremony with Randolph and his family and the Navy will take care of him. He won't get away with betraying the trust of his country and making a fool of both Randolph and me. Damn it, Anne, we trusted him!"

Anne was afraid to say anything else or hear any more. She listened and worried as Jackson explained that Randolph had gone before the I.G. and that as Jared's immediate supervisor, he had already been subpoenaed and interviewed. The military police were looking for Jared and it would behoove him not to show up to this Change of Command Ceremony.

"The plan is in place."

Anne took her phone out to text Pam in an effort check on her and make sure everything was on schedule and that she was in a good place. Pam texted back that René had shown up in Virginia Beach at the house. Anne could not believe it. Jackson gently touched the phone and shook his head. Anne knew he meant that he'd told her too much and everything he said was for her ears only.

She turned and watched the trees go by as they traveled the highway, allowing her mind to drift to over thirty-five years ago when she first met Pam and Randolph, now their dearest friends. It was a Sunday and both Randolph and Jackson were in their third year at the Naval Academy, making them Midshipmen Second Class (2/C). The guys didn't have "liberty" to go in town but they could hang out on the yard until about seven o'clock, when liberty expired. Civilians called it curfew. Anne had thought it strange that she, one so free, was entering a relationship with a man who had so much structure and such limited freedom in his world.

Anne and Pam arrived at the Naval Academy around the same time. They were meeting two "mids" for a bite to eat at Dry Dock restaurant in the basement of Dahlgren Hall. This would give them the chance to visit, even though the guys couldn't leave campus. They often laughed at the way the four of them met and all that transpired that day. It was so many years ago. Anne was wearing a red dress and she had driven to Annapolis from Baltimore, where she was a student at Grover College. She'd met Jackson a month before at a rugby game. He'd suggested she come visit that Sunday afternoon and meet him in front of Herndon.

When Anne stood at Herndon monument, she had a clear view of the Officer's Club and saw the most beautiful girl in a navy blue and white polka dotted dress with a head full of thick black hair that draped her brown shoulders. The woman, she'd later know as Pamela Sloane, stood waiting pensively as if she knew a secret that the whole world wanted to know. There was a melancholy air about her countenance that sparked Anne's curiosity. She wondered who she was and who she was meeting.

Then Jackson approached Anne in his pristine white uniform and she momentarily forgot about the young woman and focused all her attention on him. A born athlete he played basketball for Navy. The twenty-one- year old approaching her was close to 6'3" tall and handsome, confirming with his broad grin that reluctantly joining her friends at that rugby game may have been the smartest thing she ever did. She often tells him that she fell in love with him at that very moment.

They strolled over to the restaurant, careful not to touch. This meant not linking arms or even holding hands. It was considered "PDA" (public display of affection) and it was a big "no-no." After they became friends she and Pam used to tease the guys about PDA as Pam would jokingly threatened to passionately kiss Randolph in the mouth and they'd watch him back up and get away from her with a quickness. They'd all laugh, but she threatened that one day she was going to do it when he was in full dress blues or whites, in a very official place in broad daylight. She never did.

Anne remembered young Randolph and how handsome he looked in his uniform that day when the two entered Dry Dock. She was surprised to learn they were friends and company mates when Jackson got up and introduced them. They sat at a table nearby and Anne could tell without even knowing them just by their energy that both Randolph and Pam were falling in love.

She looked over at Jackson and thought how little had changed. His black curly hair had turned grey at his temples but the spark in his green eyes was still there and he was still fit and as handsome as ever. They drove along until the sign over-head read "Naval Station Norfolk," and took their place in line and waited for clearance through the security check point.

Chapter 54

....

He had once been lost. Life had shown him kindness and things changed for a while. Adopted and freed from the unintended consequences of his mother's addictions, everyone believed Mike finally had a chance. He'd "make something out of himself." Everybody likes a Cinderella story and for a minute it looked as if he was going to get to go to the ball. Except the top of the dispensary, building 8, was as far away from Sanford, Florida as you could get. It was also pretty far away from the ball and worlds away from happily ever.

As he lay flat on his belly with the cold metal trigger pressed against his finger, he worked to block thoughts of yesterday and to focus on the mission at hand. The roof- top gravel felt like so many marbles under his skin and finally his target was in sight. The pain of the thousand jagged rocks he rested on soothed him. He was about to kill a very powerful man and get away with it. Killing a man he had never met seemed worlds away from the Jefferson High School football All-American he once was.

Mike squeezed his eyes shut and tried to blink out the memories like specks of sand trapped in his eye. They burned. Remembering his adopted parents and the care they'd given him after his mother died made his skin hot even in the chill of the morning. He had discarded the plans they had for his life like yesterday's trash. That was his past. He pressed his body hard against the rocks and tightened his grip on the smooth, cold metal of the rifle, trying to escape the memories and the pile of shit that his life had reverted back to. He thought, from shit he came and to shit he returned and a low chuckle escaped his lips.

He still remembered. The house was small and the smell of lemon pie cooling in the kitchen mixed with the scent of Old Spice to create a refuge that he'd craved all his little boy life. His foster mother, Shelly, calling to him from the kitchen inviting him to taste some warm fresh baked love. She was round and soft and smelled of vanilla and sweat. She thought that pie, pudding or sponge cake could heal any pain and for a while it did.

Mike remembered Shelly and her husband Eugene saying they prayed for him for years before they knew him. Well a lot of good that did. Their God must have been hard of hearing. He knew they loved him and they tried to put him back together. But he was a broken boy when he arrived at their home. He was a broken 6-year-old who had already lived a lifetime of horror. He'd witnessed a murder and disposed of a grown man's dead body. By the time he was six years old Mike knew that a woman's body, her mouth, her butt and what was between her legs could be used and disregarded like trash. He'd watched his birth mother Ruth Anne buy, sell and trade with her flesh too many times.

He lived with Eugene and Shelly for two years before they adopted him and gave him a new name. Eugene had always wanted a son and so at the age of 8, Joe became Eugene Michael Tilman Jr. He was called "Junior" by Shelly and Eugene and "Mike" by everybody at school. In his heart, he was still Joe. It was Joe, not "Mike" steadying the gun on the rooftop and waiting for the signal to shoot.

He shook off the distraction and rebooted his mind like a reliable machine. He adjusted the scope on the AK-47 assault rifle and waited in silence for the signal Jared had instructed him he'd get.

He knew who Jared was when he'd gotten the call. It was his brother's voice. It was a call he'd waited for all of his life. But to Jared, Joe was a part of a long forgotten past. Even when they had spoken on the phone the couple of times to arrange today's hit, he couldn't bring himself to reveal his true identity. In time he would, but not yet. He'd dreamed of what that day would be like for a long time. Now he just had to wait. This one thing was standing in the way of his happiness, this one last thing.

Joe had collected news articles on Jared's career and had followed his ascension into another world, light years away from the trailer on that lone dirt road next to the trash dump. He knew about his pretty black wife and her high ranking father. He even knew where they lived and that Jared had a mistress. He knew his brother better than any other human could know him and he knew he would not be able to maintain his new life.

Joe knew that Jared would never be able to live his life without taking. He was his brother and he too, was molded by the lack and emptiness they'd suffered as boys. It motivated him to take. So taking the money for the secrets, he knew about that and could have predicted it. Taking another man's life to save his own was on today's agenda. He wasn't sure about the girl, Michelle, but Joe had seen Jared kill a man over a cat. He knew his brother well. But oddly enough, these negative traits only made him love and admire him more.

The ceremony was about to begin and within an hour he'd be rich and the world, changed forever. Joe felt an unfamiliar sense of freedom and power.

The pride he felt seeing his brother on the second row directly behind his wife and her handsome black family was unexplainable. He could tell they had not expected to see his brother Jared, because everybody looked surprised and uncomfortable when he took his seat. He was surprised to see the heavyset man and woman seated next to Jared's wife's mother and her youngest daughter. They must have been some relatives. The white Admiral with the pretty blonde in red must have been Jared's boss. They all looked pretty tense before taking their seats, all except for Jared, who looked as cool as ice and as confident as ever. Joe couldn't see their faces anymore. The national anthem was over and everyone sat down.

Jared's mark stepped to the podium accompanied by five men, completely unaware that the two lead guards were plants. Jared had paid them each $25,000. They were both married and had told their wives the huge one-time deposit was a bonus. And in some ways it was. They were about to let a man die. The CNO was on the platform, the Base Commander, Chaplain and Randolph's predecessor.

The guard on the right adjusted his earpiece. That was part one of a three-pronged signal. It was stupid. It was basic. But the mark would be shot today. Joe waited for the adjusting of the perfectly Winsor-knotted tie and the final signal, the removal of the Government Issue sunglasses. They'd been in charge of security detail and knew Joe was on the roof alone, poised to shoot. The adrenalin rush he felt was like good sex. He fired one shot and two shots followed.

Thou shall not kill.

Chapter 55

....

The crowd moved in a collective rush as Randolph fell backward and hit the ground. They got the CNO off the platform and it was cleared of dignitaries who were replaced by swarming medical personnel. Pam saw the blood stain on her husband's shoulder invade more and more of the winter blue uniform and white shirt and spread to the platform floor. She wanted to scream but she couldn't. Blood was on his face and he wasn't moving. She jumped up to run to him and felt Jackson's hand on her arm pulling her back. They were taking him away and everyone was in a panic. Rae screamed and bolted toward the podium, only to be intercepted by Anne.

"Let's get to the ambulance and go with him to the hospital, honey. Let them get him in a secure space. Come on." She calmly took Rae, who she loved as if she were her own daughter, and led her in the direction they had taken her father's limp body.

Pam looked for the rest of her family as she ran towards her husband and the waiting ambulance. Jared was gone and René, who sat directly in front of him was on the ground. Pam hadn't heard Rachel, Reagan, Trent and all of the rest of them screaming for help and trying to get her attention. Ella Jean motioned for her to go on as a group of medics finally got to René.

"We've got her, Pam. She's been shot in the arm, she gonna be alright, we'll meet you at the hospital," Ella Jean was holding on to René who was now on a stretcher.

Pam turned around, breaking free from Jackson and ran to her daughter screaming in terror.

"Who did this? Who…what…why is this happening? René! Are you okay?" She attempted to touch her daughter.

The paramedics moved her hand and René smiled a weak smile. "I'm okay, mom. Go with dad. I'm okay."

Jared headed toward the helicopter waiting on the aircraft carrier. It had been arranged before the I.G.'s boys got to everybody and it had stayed that way. By the time the military police knew it was him in the helicopter instead of the Lieutenant Commander whose identification he had stolen, doctored up and been using for the last two weeks, he would be out of the country. He had made the payments and arranged to have his bags stored on board. Jared planned to never come back. He would send for his wife or figure out a way to get her and his son to him but he knew he'd never come back.

He knew where the first shot came from but was perplexed about the other two shots he heard as he was jumping up to get out of there. He'd find out later. Right now, he just had to make sure he got safely out of the country. They would be looking for him everywhere, so he had to carefully execute his plan and use every I.D. he'd stolen or purchased along with the doctored passports. He didn't feel guilty that Randolph was dead. He felt victorious. Randolph had always been good to him but Jared could feel his disapproval right beneath the surface. The disapproval and the superiority were always there, the many questions he was too decent to ask were always there. Jared was trying to kill everything they stood for because in order for René to realize she belonged with him, that whole world she held so dear, had to be destroyed. He'd done it. He'd won.

Or so he thought.

We wrestle not against flesh and blood but against principalities and wickedness in high places.

Chapter 56

....

The sweet fragrance of a dozen vases of colorful blooms in the pale green room at Portsmouth Naval Hospital rushed toward Pam as she walked in the door.   Randolph's smile added light.

"Hey you," he grinned

The beeping of the monitor provided a cadence to the room that was soothing. The aroma was life. The room did not smell like death and the sorrow that Pam dreaded. Randolph's heart was beating steady and strong. The room was so peaceful.

His dark thick lashes framing his deep brown eyes and the laugh lines surrounding his smile only made Randolph appear more mischievous than he actually was.   His muscular body was positioned in the raised hospital bed defying his fifty-eight years. The white bandages on his left shoulder and chest peaked out from the hospital gown. Pam thought of how close the bullet came to his heart and closed her eyes to hold back the tears. It had been three days since the horrific accident.

"It appears you just can't get enough excitement, *old warrior*," she touched his hand tenderly and moved his wedding band and Naval Academy ring back and forth with her index finger. Pam drank in all of him, savoring the very sight of his warm body, of the rising and falling of his chest, signaling life. She'd feared the worst and was sure the dreams had been premonitions of his death. Instead she now felt that maybe each dream had been a promise of sorts. Perhaps they were warnings. The dead birds and the birds attacking were both warnings. She was certain of it. Then she remembered what Daddy Sloane said once, when she dreamed that he died. She had run to him in his recliner sobbing and clutching his thigh so tightly she could feel each bone and muscle.

Daddy Sloane had few vices but he religiously believed in dreams and "playing numbers," which was homegrown gambling that predated the lottery.

At the breakfast table he'd put down the newspaper and scratch his stubby chin and say, "I dreamed about fish last night- I'm a play two fives and a one, and box it."

 The morning following her dream that he was dead, he'd patted her head gently and said, "now, now, stop cryin', baby girl. Let me tell you a little bit about interpreting dreams. Things ain't always what they seem and you can't take things at face value. You got to know what it's all about underneath."

He took a worn booklet from his pocket. It read *Policy Pete's Dream Book of Numbers*. He leafed through it and explained that dreaming about a man's death usually meant that a woman would surely die.

"So, you dreaming that daddy is going to die don't mean nothing about your daddy."

Daddy Sloane was easy reassurance and his laughter was rich and soothing. She was fortunate enough to have married a man just like her daddy and he was alive. Thank God Randolph was alive. The dreams had brought her to this place. They were finally set free.

She focused her gaze on her husband, and their eyes locked.

His smile vanished as he whispered, "did they get him?"

She shook her head no.

"Let's not talk about Jared. There will be plenty of time for that. Let's get you well enough to come home. Jared won't get away with this."

She didn't mention that Jackson told her they'd discovered Jared's brother and knew that he was in on the whole thing and they'd both gotten out of the country, or that Frankie Bea had been following Jared. Pam learned that Ella Jean thought Frankie Bea had fired the two shots that grazed René's arm. They were meant to kill Jared but Frankie Bea wasn't expecting him to get up, because he hadn't discovered Jared's plan to kill Randolph. When Jared jumped up to leave, the bullet hit René who had been sitting right in front of him.

The military police lost him in the commotion of the shootings. It was a mess. Pam couldn't believe her basic boring life had come to everybody planning to kill somebody else to solve their problems or avenge a wrong. She thought it was the worst kind of evil and it didn't make sense. Frankie Bea had denied any involvement and wasn't even questioned by the police. They assumed all the shots came from the guy on the roof and were aimed at Randolph. The casings and bullets weren't found.

Pam wasn't sure how to tell her husband that René had been shot. She'd wait until he was stronger to tell him he was a grandfather too. The baby almost didn't make it. Jared and René's son's life had almost ended before it began and Jared would have to live with the fact that it was his plan that almost killed his progeny and any future he could have with him. René would survive. Tony Green was with her when Pam left her room upstairs when she'd gotten word that Randolph was awake and lucid.

The door opened and family began piling into the little room. Pam gladly included Anne and Jackson in that number, and her new brother-in-law-to-be, who she was learning to call Moses and not Reverend Franklin. Ella Jean had asked for her help to plan the holiday wedding and Randolph agreed to escort his sister-in-law down the aisle. Ella Jean and Reverend Franklin were looking at parcels of land to build their new home. Grinning, Trent and Sean approached the bed and gave a smiling Randolph a mock fraternity handshake knowing his injury wouldn't allow the real thing.

"We knew you were too ice cold to die like that," Trent grinned.

The whole room laughed at the foolishness of the compliment. Rae, Rachel and a slender Reagan who still showed no visible signs of pregnancy, stood near their dad feeling thankful for the love that nurtured them and still existed in their family.

Pam realized at that moment that she was stronger than she ever thought possible; there were some things, including her spirit, that were unbreakable. Nothing could change that: not pills, neither power nor privilege could break her. She was whole, still standing, despite a mother like Jean Washington Sloane and all that Pam had endured. She and those she loved could never by broken man, the likes of Jared Foster Reed.

The force and strength of the United States Navy, the determination of her husband and that of their friend Jackson was time tested. The love that bonded her, Ella Jean and her daughters to each other had no end. It was far more than a bullet could destroy. Greed and pain would never triumph over that which was hers and knowing this assured her that the battle was far from over.

The End

*The Lord is not slow in keeping his **promises**, as some understand slowness.*

2 Peter 3:9

Book Club Study Guide

1. What is Pamela Sloane Hamilton's driving motivation?
2. What is Ella Jean's driving motivation?
3. Do the two intersect? What are their similarities and differences in what they seek and/or need?
4. Who is your favorite character in the book and why?
5. Which character provoked the strongest negative emotions and why?
6. Who should René end up with as a life mate?
7. Do you think Randolph will retire after this?
8. Will Jared return for his son and if so, what do you think will happen?
9. What got Pamela off of the pills almost cold turkey?
10. Explain the dreams and dead birds and what you think they meant for each character.
11. How were socio economic differences depicted in the book?
12. How was love depicted in the story and how many different types and languages of love do you find?
13. What does the book present to the readers on the relations between siblings in the story?
14. How does Ella Jean keep from allowing victimization to characterize her? How is she not a victim?
15. Should there be another Promises book? What do you want to know?